A DRAGON'S GUIDE to making PERFECT WISHES

A DRAGON'S GUIDE to MAKING PERFECT WISHES

Book 3

Laurence Yep & Joanne Ryder

Illustrations by Mary GrandPré

CROWN BOOKS
FOR YOUNG READERS
NEW YORK

Text copyright © 2017 by Laurence Yep and Joanne Ryder
Jacket art and interior illustrations copyright © 2017 by Mary GrandPré

All rights reserved. Published in the United States by Crown Books for Young Readers, an imprint of Random House Children's Books, a division of Penguin Random House LLC, New York.

Crown and the colophon are registered trademarks of Penguin Random House LLC.

Visit us on the Web! randomhousekids.com

Educators and librarians, for a variety of teaching tools, visit us at RHTeachersLibrarians.com

Library of Congress Cataloging-in-Publication Data
Names: Yep, Laurence, 1948– author. | Ryder, Joanne, author. |
GrandPré, Mary, illustrator.
Title: A dragon's guide to making perfect wishes / Laurence Yep & Joanne Ryder; illustrations by Mary GrandPré.
Description: First edition. | New York: Crown Books for Young Readers, [2017] |
Series: A dragon's guide; book 3 | Summary: Winnie and her pet dragon Miss Drake are back to their lessons as they head to the 1915 San Francisco World's Fair and wish-granting souvenirs follow them home.
Identifiers: LCCN 2016016159 (print) | LCCN 2016047444 (ebook) |
ISBN 978-0-385-39236-5 (hardback) | ISBN 978-0-385-39237-2 (hardcover library binding) | ISBN 978-0-385-39238-9 (ebook)
Subjects: | CYAC: Dragons—Fiction. | Magic—Fiction. | Wishes—Fiction. | Time travel—Fiction. | BISAC: JUVENILE FICTION / Fantasy & Magic. | JUVENILE FICTION / Animals / Mythical. | JUVENILE FICTION / Humorous Stories.
Classification: LCC PZ7.Y44 Dqrj 2017 (print) | LCC PZ7.Y44 (ebook) |
DDC [Fic]—dc23

Printed in the United States of America
10 9 8 7 6 5 4 3 2 1
First Edition

To Kathy Gilmartin, whose notes got me through
Miss Havisham's interior decorating, and to her father,
that old San Franciscan, William Gilmartin, who survived
the Earthquake and went to the Exposition

CHAPTER ONE

⟨✦⟩

It is vital to teach your pet that the past is never past.
It's just hiding, waiting to surprise or catch you unawares.

∽ MISS DRAKE ∽

"Wake up! Wake up! Wake up!" Winnie bellowed.

I roused enough to realize that my bed was creaking and shaking like it wanted to throw me off. I'd woken just the same way more than a hundred years ago to death and devastation. With a chill, I thought, *Earthquake!*

With my eyes only half-opened, I forced myself to sit up, knowing that we had only seconds to reach the safety of the doorframe. That was when I saw that a more personal force of nature was trying to demolish my bed. Clad in pajamas and bathrobe and flinging her arms every which way, my pet, Winnie, was bouncing up and down on the mattress like a jack-in-the-box gone mad. She was making up in energy what she lacked in destructive size and weight.

I lunged forward and caught her in midair between my paws. "Stop that! Who asked you to replace my alarm clock?" I glanced groggily at the clock and gave a start. It was before sunrise!

I had grown resigned to Winnie invading my apartment at all hours, but this was the first time she'd come in so early. Hatchlings need to learn that there are boundaries they must not cross, but lately I'd been lax about disciplining her.

"Humans should never be seen nor heard before the first cup of tea," I said in a voice stern enough to make tigers cower and sharks flee.

Winnie, though, simply kicked her feet slowly back and forth as she dangled between my paws. "But it's Topsy-Turvy Day!"

Topsy-Turvy Day was a tradition at Winnie's school, the Spriggs Academy. On that day, the magical and natural students switched places—*naturals* was another word for humans in the magical community. Magicals had to stay in their human disguises and use no magic. Naturals had to wear masks of magical creatures and perform simple coin or card tricks. If a magical was caught using magic or a natural flubbed the trick, the miscreant had to sing the Academy fight song three times in a minute or suffer further penalties.

I set her on my bed so I could cover my muzzle politely with a paw as I yawned. "Topsy-Turvy Day was last week, and anyway that's for Spriggs, not home."

She wrapped her arms around my foreleg. "It was so much fun at school, I thought we'd start holding it here."

Gently, I pushed her aside and began re-coiling myself elegantly on my large, round, oh-so-comfortable bed. "You already had plenty of fun yesterday setting off fireworks on Vesuvius."

It had seemed like a pleasant thing to do after picnicking on the volcano's slopes as we gazed at Naples's sunny bay. How was I supposed to know the pyrotechnics would cause a small panic in the city below?

Winnie threw herself on my moving tail, pinning it against the mattress. "But that was yesterday, and today's today. I want every day to be Topsy-Turvy from now on."

There was only one way I was going to keep her from

attaching herself to me like a barnacle. "No wish is perfect, so we'll only celebrate it today. We'll begin at nine."

Winnie jutted out her chin like she did when she was driving one of her hard bargains. "Eight." She seemed determined to enjoy as much of the day as possible.

"Eight-thirty," I countered.

"Deal." Releasing my tail, she clambered over my coiled body and lay down in the empty center of my bed. Before I could tell her to stop treating me like her personal jungle gym, she had curled up against me as if my scales were soft as wool.

I should, of course, have picked her up and set her outside. I should have done many things to educate this half-feral creature, but as so often happened, I found myself indulging her.

Sheltered within the armored circle of my body, she was already falling asleep. As I listened to her breathing slow and deepen, I was touched by her faith in me to keep her safe.

In her brief ten years, she'd led a hard, stressful life, staying one step ahead of the detectives and lawyers seeking to take her away from her mother and send her to her cold, unfeeling grandfather Jarvis. But those days were gone.

My Fluffy, Winnie's great-aunt, had left the mansion

and her wealth to Liza, Winnie's mother. But even without the house and fortune, Winnie knew I would protect her from harm, be it from an army of detectives, lawyers, or three-headed monsters.

With one forepaw, I lifted her head up, and with my other forepaw, I got a pillow and eased it between her cheek and my body.

Since Winnie came into my life, every day has been topsy-turvy, I reflected as I fell asleep again.

I'm afraid it was eight-forty-five before I woke up again. Lifting my head carefully, I saw that Winnie was gone, so I uncoiled from my pest-free bed and stretched leisurely.

After taking care of my morning toilet, I thought I had done well to climb the basement stairs by nine.

"Ha! You're late!" Winnie scolded.

Fluffy had taught me the Topsy-Turvy chant when you demanded a magic trick from a natural:

"Magic, magic all around.

Have you lost it? Or is it found?"

Winnie held up a right hand and pulled back her sleeve. "Observe. Nothing up my sleeve." She repeated the same gesture with her left. "And nothing here."

Before Topsy-Turvy Day at Spriggs, she'd used on-line videos to learn how to produce pennies from behind a spectator's ear. So I expected her to take a coin from behind one of mine, and I was about to tell her, "No pennies, please. A dragon deserves only quarters or higher denominations."

But instead, an orange water pistol appeared in her hand.

I wagged a finger at her. "Don't you dare—*glug!*"

With alarming accuracy, she sent a stream of water into my mouth and up my face. For such a small pistol, it held an amazing amount of water. This would not have been a problem in my dragon form, but for Topsy-Turvy Day, I'd changed into a human disguise. Instantly, I felt my coiffure sag and the wet locks fall around my ears like a sand castle collapsing in the incoming tide. I'd have to redo the whole spell again. Give me my scales and a can of expensive car wax anytime.

That was annoying enough, but then I saw some of the water had splashed off me and onto Caleb's portrait.

"Have more respect for your great-grandfather," I scolded, pointing to the drops of liquid.

"The painting's covered by glass." Winnie held up the orange pistol. "And anyway, it's only water. I'm cleaning it."

I was about to unleash a blistering scolding when I caught myself in time. *Control yourself. She doesn't understand. Patience is the key to raising a pet, especially a natural hatchling. And before you lecture or punish her, you must explain what she has done wrong.*

"Would you shoot water at a picture of your mother or your great-aunt Amelia?" I demanded as I rubbed the glass vigorously with a dress sleeve.

"Well, no." She gave a shrug. "That'd be like shooting water right at them."

I lowered my arm as the full truth dawned on me. "But Caleb is just a name to you, isn't he?"

Winnie shrugged. "What do you expect? He was Great-Aunt Amelia's dad. I never met him, and he never wrote me like she did. How could he? He died before I was born."

Her grandfather Jarvis had chased her for years, trying to get custody of her, and that had made her suspicious of strangers. Acquaintances had to prove to her that they were worthy of her friendship either in person like her schoolmates or at least in letters and gifts like Fluffy, my dear pet Amelia. To that small circle, Winnie was intensely loyal, but to everyone else—including her own ancestors, it seemed—she was intensely indifferent.

She watched water drip from Caleb's picture.

"Besides, one Granddad Jarvis is enough. I don't need to meet his father."

Last Christmas, Jarvis had given up trying to get Winnie because, as he told her, she was already as tough and ruthless as he was. Though I'd done my best to comfort her, that thought still festered inside her and apparently was another reason she wanted to ignore her family's past. "He was also the father of your great-aunt Amelia, who was the kindest of souls," I tried to clarify.

She turned away from Caleb. "I'm okay with the way things are."

Winnie was like a castaway on her own lonely little island who saw Caleb only at a distance across a vast sea of time. But with my long life, my memories stretched from one pet to the next like a bridge connecting one island after another.

"Well, he thought enough of you to leave you something." I smoothed my wet bangs from my eyes. "I'd intended to give it to you at the end of the year, but I think we need to do it sooner."

Winnie's eyes widened. "He knew about me?"

"It was more a hope," I admitted truthfully. "Everyone was making a time capsule then, so he did too, and he asked me to hand it to his descendants after a hundred years."

Winnie had the courtesy to look a little guilty. "What's in the time capsule?"

"I don't know any more than you do," I said. "He filled the time capsule and locked it before he gave it and its key to me."

Winnie's eyebrows shot up excitedly. "Do you think there's any treasure in it?"

"It would be what an eleven-year-old boy thought of as treasures," I cautioned. "But maybe what he put in there will make your ancestor seem more real to you."

Unfortunately, though, his youthful tastes were only a small part of the delight that had been Caleb. He would never be alive to Winnie as he was to me. He'd been only three when the Great Earthquake hit San Francisco, and I'd carried him from the ruins of the original house.

But Winnie hadn't held him tight as the wall of fire swept across San Francisco after the earthquake, the smoke turning day into night.

Then I remembered an invitation I'd gotten. With regret, I'd torn it up. But now . . . yes, why not? "In fact, would you like to meet him Saturday?"

"In a magic mirror?" Winnie asked.

I shook my head. Magic mirrors are notoriously uncooperative, rarely showing you what you want to see in the past. "I've tried looking for Caleb in several mirrors, but none of them would let me. No, we'll go back to see him in person."

Winnie gasped. "You mean, time travel?"

"Of a sort," I said. "The High Council has set up rules so no one can change the past and our present."

"Could we really do something to change the present?" Winnie asked with a bit too much curiosity.

"Not if we follow the Council's rules . . . which we certainly will do," I told her firmly. But I thought to myself, *More or less.*

I began making mental lists of all the things I needed to do now, starting with RSVPing to Willamar, a respectable troll who was arranging the excursion. I had some lovely gold-edged note cards that a young Queen Victoria had given me after I'd fetched the perfect Norwegian fir tree for her husband, Prince Albert, one Christmas. She knew he was homesick during the holidays, so she'd hoped that he would cheer up if they decorated a tree like families did in his homeland. Who knew a German custom would catch on in England?

And since we had to go in period outfits, I'd have to obtain something suitable yet striking for Winnie and myself. And of course, there were our hairdos to plan and appropriate accessories to unearth in my closet. How delightful!

"Time traveling is even better than Topsy-Turvy Day," Winnie crowed, and gave me another squirt of water.

As water dripped from my nose, I held up a hand and announced, "And with that prank, I now declare Topsy-Turvy Day officially over for the year."

"But—" Winnie began.

I waved my finger in front of her face. "No ifs, ands, or buts. I have a lot to do if we're going to be ready by Friday."

Winnie tapped her water pistol against her chin. "Well, I guess there's always next year."

With a pet, there is always a surprise to look forward to . . . and a surprise to dread.

CHAPTER TWO

Time travel is never easy. If you want a carefree trip,
take a walk in the park.

MISS DRAKE

The cab let us off in front of a four-story mansion that had been built a year after the Exposition had closed. It was surrounded by large block-like modern homes and apartment houses, jammed together with immaculate sidewalks where not a weed was allowed to grow. It was all very impersonal, very sterile, and very expensive.

Winnie was wearing what a well-dressed young lady would

in 1915 . . . which did not please her at all. Luckily she could wear a long jacket that would cover some of her lovely dress and keep her warm when the fog blew in. I offered to form her untamable hair into charming dangling ringlets for the evening, but she refused. So her wide-brimmed hat sat a bit crooked on top of her curls. And I skipped the silk parasol entirely. A girl of 1915 would think it an accessory, but Winnie would consider it a handy weapon. Not a perfect transformation, but I did my best.

As she headed toward the party, her walk wasn't any different than it usually was. But her 1915 skirt and petticoats were made for flouncing.

She scowled down at it. "This dress is just too girly. And why do I need gloves? It's not cold."

"Remember, it's 1915. A proper young lady wears gloves in public," I told her. "And besides it will cover up your ring. I wouldn't want some envious guest to snatch it off your finger."

I had given Winnie her ring last Christmas. Anyone could see the gem change color from purplish red in candlelight to greenish blue in daylight. But it had other qualities that only she would discover in time . . . if she didn't lose it first.

"Time travel is not without its penalties," I replied, and shooed her along.

After the Great Earthquake and Fire had destroyed much of San Francisco in 1906, the city had wanted to show the world that it had risen again from the ashes. San Francisco had used the opening of the Panama Canal as an excuse, but by 1915, the Panama-Pacific International Exposition had become so much more. It was a place of wonder and delight: the San Francisco we saw with our hearts rather than our eyes had become real.

About a hundred years later, fans of that incredible event had created a club, the Fellowship of the Jewel City, and were traveling through time to a special day there.

For the trip, the members would all wear clothing suitable to that era, and Clipper had had just the outfits for us at her traveling emporium.

When I joined Winnie on the porch, I checked my own ensemble. I was wearing a stylish green wool jacket, V-neck silk blouse, and pleated skirt, short enough to show off my dainty ankles. I had finished my outfit with a matching green hat set at a jaunty tilt. My long red hair was fashioned into a smooth bun on my head, the latest chignon style.

It was a shame that Winnie's mother, Liza, couldn't be here. We were becoming more comfortable with one another, so I knew she liked dressing up for Halloween.

She would have enjoyed seeing Winnie in her costume and wearing one herself.

But Liza was on a trail ride, organized by her employer, Rhiannon. A group of horseback riders followed the route of a cattle drive from long ago—though without the cows. Liza would be gone about a week and was without a cell phone just like all the other riders. So I was in loco parentis.

Winnie's hand hesitated before pressing the doorbell. "Can we go in now?" she asked.

I took a breath and then exhaled slowly. "Let's enjoy the calm before the storm just a moment longer."

Winnie looked behind us toward the street. "Storm? What storm?"

"A storm of very hot air signifying nothing," I said, and nodded for Winnie to ring the doorbell. "Though the Fellowship was organized by lovers of the Exposition, they've developed an obsession with a carved pendant of a golden mongoose. It clutched to its chest the fabled ruby, the Heart of Kubera. Legend says it was created by a great sorcerer and sometimes grants its owner incredible riches like the way Kubera, the Hindu god of wealth, does. Though its last owner, Lady Gravelston, was already so wealthy, she didn't need magic to make her very, very rich.

Winnie was curious as most people were when they first heard about it. "Where is it now? Maybe we can fly there to see it on our next adventure."

"No one knows where it is," I said while we waited. "It disappeared in front of hundreds of people during a ball that was held at the Exposition for Lady Gravelston."

I heard heavy footsteps, and then a Viking warrior in evening wear opened the door. His blond pigtails hung down all the way to the tails of his dress coat. Like other trolls I knew, when he disguised himself as a natural, Willamar chose the handsomest one he could find. A gathering of disguised trolls was like a beauty contest.

Willamar leaned over to peer at my disguise. "We're missing one very important partygoer. Would you be . . ."

"Yes, I'm Miss Drake," I said.

Willamar engulfed my hand in both of his and bowed several times as he drew me inside. "Thank you for finally honoring the Fellowship of the Jewel City with your presence."

"And who's this?" Willamar drew his eyebrows together and then brightened. "Oh, you must be the great-niece of—"

I cut him off before he could blurt the word *Fluffy*, the nickname that I'd given Winnie's great-aunt.

"Yes—Amelia. Willamar, let me introduce you to Winifred Burton."

Willamar nodded to Winnie. "Your great-aunt was such a charming and compassionate lady. We all miss her."

"Thank you," she said. I was glad to see she was on her best behavior tonight.

As Willamar led us down the hallway, I felt I was already journeying through time. The wallpaper could have been from any mansion of the day. Inside the ornate sconces, the electric lightbulbs had the shape of gas-jet flames. Most houses of the period were still using gas to light their interiors. Only the very wealthy would have electrified their homes.

The large parlor had double sliding doors, and the chandelier above us had additional fake gaslights pouring light down on the costumed crowd.

"Everybody's a natural?" Winnie asked, looking around.

"No, the High Council insisted on a number of conditions for this trip," Willamar explained. "All magicals must wear human shapes just in case something goes wrong."

"Oh, like when my magical friends are outside of Spriggs," Winnie said.

Also like Spriggs, the Fellowship was a microcosm of the magical community itself, with members from most of the magical clans. Even with my dull human snout, I caught a whiff of zombie, centaur, sylph, and a dozen others as they crowded around. It was a measure of how popular the Exposition had been with magicals as well as naturals.

Even so, I couldn't help marveling. "Time travel always makes the High Council nervous. It's a miracle they ever agreed."

"I thank the mystique that has grown about the Heart of Kubera," Willamar said. "Several councilors who belong to the Fellowship are as curious as I about what happened to the gem."

He waved to a mousy woman I did not recognize. Her white blouse was plain, and so was her brown skirt and heavy coat. Her black hat was unadorned and a bit frumpy

From ten yards away, I thought she was in her fifties, but as I got closer, I saw the tightness in the skin of her face, contrasting with her deeply veined and wrinkled hands. Hands rarely lie.

I upped my estimate of her age to seventy-five or perhaps eighty. She was a natural who used a plastic surgeon rather than the nuisance of magical potions every day to keep her looking young.

"Lorelei, here's someone I know you'll want to meet." Willamar turned to us. "Lorelei was the driving force behind this evening's trip."

She flattered me by placing a palm beneath her throat as if feeling faint. "Not *the* Miss Drake," she gushed. "I am such an admirer of yours."

"I'm pleased to meet—" I began when a parasol shoved Lorelei to the side.

"Do not monopolize our gues' of honor, my dear," said a woman with a thick accent as she slipped into the space her parasol had produced. She was wearing a rose outfit, complete with matching floral hat and parasol, but I've never encountered a magical spell that could completely disguise a werewolf because even the strongest spells can't mask their musky scent. "Miss Drake, were you at t'e Hall when t'e t'ief took t'e Heart of Kubera?"

"Lady Luminita," I said, dipping my head slightly. "My friend Caleb and I had seen it earlier, and on that night he was more interested in buying souvenirs."

"Well, who do you think—?" Lorelei began to ask.

Raising her voice, Silana Voisin spoke over Lorelei. "What a pity you weren't there, Miss Drake. You might have recognized the thief because only a magical would have the skills and knowledge to steal the Heart of Kubera."

She was wearing a long black traveling dress with plum

lace and a veiled hat that was the height of fashion . . . in 1914. Unfortunately, we were traveling to 1915, where people in the know would recognize her outfit as *so* last year. But then Silana always shot short of the mark just like she always came in second-best at the Magic contest during the Enchanters' Fair.

I thought Silana had been rude to Lorelei, especially after she had helped arrange this trip. So I was going to ask Lorelei to finish her thought, but she had hunched her shoulders and bent her head meekly as if she was used to fading into the background, the perpetual wallflower. I felt rather sorry for her.

"No, no," Willamar insisted, "the High Council investigated the theft and exonerated all the magicals at the ball. It has to be Senator Bradley, her dance partner."

Willamar, Silana, and Lady Luminita each defended their candidate for the thief. Poor Lorelei stood to the side, waiting to express her opinion but never getting a chance.

"Come," I whispered to Winnie. "They've forgotten all about us." I guided her through the clumps of other club members, all of whom were arguing about who the thief might be, like dogs chewing on the same bone.

Winnie pressed herself against me, shouting to make

herself heard over the loud debate. "I see what you mean about the storm."

Finally, we retreated to a quiet corner where Sir Isaac Newton had also taken refuge.

"Thank you for gracing our little soiree, Miss Drake." Ever the gentleman, Sir Isaac doffed his red peaked cap to me and then to Winnie. "And the ever-inquisitive Burton."

He was Winnie's immortal science teacher at the Spriggs Academy, and for this occasion, he'd given up his usual coat and knee breeches for blue trousers with a broad yellow stripe, and a scarlet jacket with enough braid to outfit a troop of hussars. Instead of boots, though, he wore an unmilitary pair of shoes with gold buckles and thick high heels.

But shoes like his had once been all the rage toward the end of Charles II's reign, when the male courtiers had to race in the audience hall, and bets were made on who would be the first of the tottering competitors to fall.

So I wouldn't have chosen Sir Isaac's shoes as the sensible walking pair suggested by Willamar's invitation. But when you have lived three centuries, I suppose you can master anything, even what was actually a pair of short stilts.

"Behold, Burton." Sir Isaac's eyes glittered with excitement as he opened one of the two lids of a small wicker basket. Inside was a squarish camera. "I intend to record every moment of the ball for examination in slow motion."

I shut the lid quickly before any of the Council members here could see it. "You'll get in trouble if you bring that into the past," I whispered in warning.

"Worry not. No mortal of the time will know. I have permission to solve a century-old mystery." Sir Isaac patted the basket affectionately.

"But you have that little machine that lets you open holes into another time," Winnie said. "Couldn't you have used that?"

"I've tried, Burton, but could never see the thief," Sir Isaac said. "So I've come to the conclusion that I must be there in person."

"How nice to see you, Miss Drake," Lady Louhi said. She was a witch who taught students about the culture and history of magicals at the Spriggs Academy. "And how lovely you look, Winnie. Oh, dear, but such a sour face. Is your stomach bothering you? I'm sure I have some peppermints." She searched her handbag, while her belongings clinked and rattled inside.

"Thank you, but there's no need," I said. "It's wearing 1915 fashion rather than a bad shrimp that's bothering Winnie." I added, "I didn't know you and Sir Isaac were members of the Fellowship."

"No, but we love solving puzzles, so Willamar invited us." Lady Louhi touched her large handbag. "Sir Isaac and I have a wager on whether his science or my magic will solve the theft."

Next to her was a boy who looked older than Winnie. He was wearing a knee-length tan leather coat with matching aviator's cap and a pair of goggles dangling around his neck. He stood so straight, I would have said he was a soldier, and his spindly arms ended in fingers that twisted like the roots of a banyan tree. So I assumed he was some sort of dryad like Paradise, our gardener—and yet his face seemed vaguely familiar, though I couldn't quite place him.

The boy was looking around the room, his sky-blue eyes darting, as if putting a price tag on everything and everyone.

"Winnie, Miss Drake, this is my nephew, Rowan," said Lady Louhi. "He goes to Powell Prep."

"Hi," Winnie said. "I go to the Spriggs Academy. We're your sister school."

He glanced at her as if she were an annoying fly buzzing around his head. "Since Powell is older, richer, and more famous, Spriggs is more like our poor cousin than a little sister."

Since Lady Louhi taught at Spriggs, I waited for her to put the brat in his place, but she simply gripped her nephew's shoulder. "Rowan, remember what I said about manners?"

Rowan, though, leaned his head to the side as he studied me curiously. "I heard you're one of those fire-breathing dragons. Or is that just gossip?"

"If you'll stand in front of something inexpensive," I suggested with a tight smile, "I'll be happy to demonstrate."

Rowan glanced around. "Everything looks way too overpriced here."

"How unfortunate," I observed.

Hastily, Lady Louhi began to shove him away. "Have I shown you the Novagems?"

"Yes," Rowan said.

"Then I'll show them to you again," she insisted.

When aunt and nephew disappeared among the club members, Winnie muttered, "I heard the boys from Powell were spoiled. Now I know it."

"What do you think?" I asked her. "Would carbonizing him spoil everyone's evening or improve it?"

"They'd choose charcoal," Winnie growled. "Definitely charcoal."

Bless Winnie's savage little heart. I could always depend on her to make the right choice.

CHAPTER THREE

~~~

Past tense and future tense are not just parts of speech.
Traveling through time is always tense.

⤳ MISS DRAKE ⤳

Lady Louhi wisely kept her nephew at a distance from us, so he avoided being turned into charcoal briquettes. Instead, Winnie and I enjoyed Willamar's buffet table and admired his chandelier.

Winnie stood right under it as she craned her neck to look up high. "I've never seen one decorated with gems."

I gazed at several hundred multicolored circles of glass sparkling above us.

"Those are the jewels from the Jewel City, Winnie," I told her with a smile. "They were called the Novagems. At the center of the fair was a building that rose to a tall tower—the Tower of Jewels—and more than a hundred thousand faceted glass gems swung in the breeze, sparkling in the day and gleaming at night under special lights. Willamar must have hunted these down and had this chandelier made to showcase them. Just splendid."

"I love your costume," Winnie said to a young woman wearing a striking headdress and carrying a tray of Scottish biscuits called scones and tiny cakes shaped like roses. I remembered they were a favorite treat at the fair.

"Thank you," said the girl. "I am supposed to be . . . like her." She pointed across the room to one of Willamar's treasures. The sculpture was ten feet tall. A tall, lovely maiden in a flowing sheer outfit raised her arms to circle her head. A large pointed star framed her face. From each tip dangled a small Novagem.

"Oh, I like her," said Winnie. "She looks like a rock star."

"She's a star maiden," I told her, "not a rock star . . . and she came first. There were nearly a hundred maidens, but they must be rarer than rare now. We'll see the lovely ladies later near the Tower of Jewels."

"Cool," Winnie said, looking more like her happy, curious self as she peered at framed newspaper articles on the wall. The theft of the Heart of Kubera had made headlines around the world, so there were front-page articles from London, Paris, Cairo, Shanghai, Rio de Janeiro, as well as New York.

Winnie studied the pictures of the pendant of the golden mongoose with the ruby in its chest. "The photos are only black and white."

"There weren't color photos yet unless someone tinted them by hand," I explained.

Winnie straightened up when she finished examining a photograph. "Even in black and white, it's still quite a rock."

"Once again, your gift for understatement underwhelms me." I sighed.

A moment later, Willamar called loudly for attention. "We've spent many meetings debating who stole the Heart of Kubera and how it was done, but tonight we finally put the question to rest." He signed to a servant who unfolded a tall, five-paneled Chinese lacquered screen. Others carried various magical apparatus behind it.

When the servants were done, they formed a wall on either side of the screen, each holding a long pole with a bright red flag and carrying a bulging pack strapped to their shoulders.

"My apologies to my thaumaturgical colleagues,"

Lady Louhi explained to the rest of the crowd, "but the High Council has insisted that no one see the enchantment." And she stepped behind the screen.

"And while Lady Louhi is preparing the spell, Miss Lorelei will entertain us with songs from the Exposition." With a bow, Willamar stepped aside, and Miss Lorelei took his place.

Her outfit looked drab compared to everyone else's, but for once it was this wallflower's chance to shine. Clasping her hands in front of her stomach, she began to sing in a pleasant soprano.

The music carried me back to the heady days while we worked to make the Exposition happen—from the wealthy folk like Winnie's great-great-grandfather, Sebastian, to the laborers who built the beautiful city within a city. But that was nothing compared to the campaign to get people to visit the incredible place we had created. Every San Franciscan—from children like Caleb to gray-haired grannies—wrote postcards to family and friends around the world, inviting them here. And come they did, arriving by ship and railroad, by buggy and on foot.

I and other San Franciscans had felt like the hosts of a giant yearlong party for the rest of America and many other countries. While World War I raged in Europe and the Near East, San Francisco had seemed like the one patch of sanity in a world gone insane. People were meant to enjoy life and one another instead of killing strangers by the thousands.

But even while I was tapping my foot in time to the music, I saw Winnie yawn. Though I was familiar with the music from that era, it was too strange and slow for her.

"Stop that," I hissed softly.

"I can't help it," Winnie said. "It's so warm in here, and I ate too much." Her jaw stretched in a bone-cracking yawn. I was going to tell her to stop distending her mouth like an anaconda, but her head was already drooping against me. She must really have been tired, so I put an arm around her instead. "Do you want to go home?"

Her head shot up. "No, no, after putting up with all this, I want to see the Exposition."

Unfortunately, I think Lorelei had noticed Winnie yawning because when she finished, she threw an angry look at my pet. I thought of having Winnie apologize to her, but at that moment, a servant came over to us with two badges. "Your travel charms, ma'am and miss."

The badges consisted of pins with the club's name, from which hung an oval token picturing the Tower of Jewels and red, white, and blue ribbons. "Please wait until Mr. Willamar tells you to put them on."

When everyone had a badge, Willamar motioned to

the screen. "My thanks to Lady Louhi for making the travel charms that will make sure we won't change the past."

Lady Louhi looked at us over the top of the screen. "The charms will put you a few nanoseconds ahead in time and space of your surroundings. The advantage is that you won't be seen or touched. The drawback is that you won't be able to touch or pick up anything. But I've adjusted the spell so you can see and hear what's happening around you. And you'll feel the cold and the heat." She added with a smile, "And though you can't really touch anyone, others may feel your presence."

Clever, clever Lady Louhi. I would never have thought of magic like that—or had the knowledge and ability to create it.

"If people in this time can't see me, I could have worn my regular clothes," Winnie complained to me.

"Our costumes will get us in the mood," I said. "Think of it like Halloween."

"But now I won't be able to get a present for Mom." Winnie sighed.

"I think she would prefer you didn't alter time to giving her a souvenir towel," I observed.

In front of us, Willamar held up his arms. "It's time to put your charms on."

I fixed Winnie's badge to her jacket and then put on mine. When the others had done the same, Lady Louhi murmured a word that must have activated them because the room shimmered for a moment. Winnie reached for a chair, but instead of grabbing it, her hand went right through it. "Whoa, it's like being a ghost."

I reached over and tapped Winnie's arm experimentally. "Did you feel that?"

"I guess we can touch one another," Winnie said.

"Now, a warning." Lady Louhi sounded like a teacher with an unruly group of children. "Be sure to stick with the group because there is a time limit on the spell. But if you get separated, you must be here by midnight to return to our own time. If you're late, you'll be stranded in the past, and your badges will no longer hide you."

"The High Council wouldn't leave us there," Silana objected. "They'd send a rescue party for us."

"Yes," Lady Louhi said, and added ominously, "and then there would be consequences."

I was sure those "consequences" would be more severe than slaps on the wrists. The High Council would send their own enforcers—but not to rescue so much as to minimize any damage the tardy one might have caused to the time stream. Inconveniencing others was one thing; endangering all of time was quite another.

Willamar was quick to keep the mood a cheerful one. "But that's not going to happen because we are all going to stay as a group."

Lady Louhi dropped back behind the screen, and a moment later, the air began to tingle. Wisps of hair got loose from Winnie's hairdo and swayed from side to side like trees in the wind. Sparks began to dance across my scales in response to the potent magic Lady Louhi was creating.

Suddenly I felt like I was being turned inside out and then back again. I checked on Winnie. She was looking a little green but determined to stand on her own.

Before I could ask her if she was all right, screen, floor, walls and the entire house vanished, and we were standing in the open air on a sandy empty lot with the sun at its apex overhead. Though we had left Willamar's mansion at night, it was now midafternoon. We were on the same spot but in 1915.

There were several houses and stores already on both sides of the street, but most of it was empty sand and weeds. These lots had been divided with stakes and cord. As valuable as this area became in Winnie's time, it wasn't very desirable now. The land was prone to flooding, and parts could become marshy. So in the years after the earthquake and fire, it had become a convenient spot to dump the debris.

Winnie glanced up at the sky. "When we went to the party, it was already evening, but now it's the afternoon again."

Winnie's hair had become even messier in traveling through time. I smoothed it down and straightened her hat as best I could with my hand. "An enchanter as skillful as Lady Louhi can travel to any day and hour. This way we'll have more time at the Exposition."

Right in front of us was a river of excited people heading in the same direction, many in horse-drawn buggies, bicycles, automobiles, and open-sided trucks with signs that said SHUTTLE and many more on foot.

Nostalgia cloaks the less pleasant memories, so I'd forgotten that sometimes the Exposition was too popular. It seemed like everybody in San Francisco was trying to get to the fair right now. The pedestrians got in the way of the vehicles, so everyone was reduced to a slow crawl.

In the meantime, behind us, Willamar's servants had stacked up their backpacks. One of them was taking goodies from them and setting them on a canvas picnic-style so we could eat and drink upon our return. The other servants circled around the club members and hoisted their flags up high to form a border around us.

Willamar flung his hand up in a grand flourish and shouted like a circus ringmaster, "Ladies, gentlemen, and sentients, I give you 1915! Welcome to the greatest World's Fair and the most mystifying theft of all time!"

Stepping off the curb, Willamar led the way with Lady Louhi on one side and Sir Isaac on the other. Winnie gave a little cry as they disappeared under 1,200 pounds of metal but after the Ford Model T chugged on, they stood unharmed in the road.

"Q.E.D.," Sir Isaac declared to the fellowship. "We are as safe as my esteemed colleague promised."

We surged after them as a group with Winnie and I walking straight through a family of four. A little girl giggled, wriggling happily from her shoulders down to her toes. And I felt a pleasant sensation as if a giant feather was tickling my insides. Well, Lady Louhi was right, our presence could certainly be felt.

"Cool," Winnie said. "It's fun being a ghost." She thrust her arm experimentally into a big man carrying a chunky box camera. When he started chuckling, she walked next to him so she could keep twirling her arm inside him. The chuckling turned into laughs and then body-shaking guffaws. People turned to stare at him.

While tears rolled down his cheek, he roared, "I don't know what's gotten into me."

It was literally an imp named Winnie.

"It's impolite to torment someone when you haven't

been properly introduced," I said, forcing Winnie's arm to her side.

"I made him laugh. That's not torment," Winnie argued, but she kept her arm down.

Since we could move through solid objects and people, we could walk at a faster pace than the crowd. Anticipating the fun of the fair, they were cheerful to begin with, but when the club passed through them, they even became merrier. You could have tracked us by the path of laughter we left behind us.

Still, it was easy to lose sight of our fellow time travelers. While we stayed with the flags, we would be walking with the rest of the club. But the servants holding the flags would also keep us together as a group. It was probably another one of the High Council's conditions for this trip.

The only problem was that the Heart of Kubera was stolen at the same moment that Caleb would be shopping for souvenirs at a kiosk, and the spots were far away from one another. However, the High Council hadn't ordered me to stay with the Fellowship, so it couldn't punish me for leaving the group and showing Winnie her ancestor.

I came up with an idea, but I had to give Winnie a choice. "We need to make a decision quick," I told her. "Do you want to try to catch the thief who took the

Heart of Kubera, or do you want to meet your great-grandfather?"

Winnie thought for a moment. "The Fellowship's got me sort of curious about the thief now." My pet was learning to read my moods a little. "But you want to see Great-Granddad, don't you?"

"Yes," I admitted, "but this trip is for you. So don't try to please me. I want to do what you want."

She bit her lip. "I guess I'm still more curious about my great-granddad."

I clasped her hand tighter, both relieved and grateful. "Then walk at the same pace I do."

When I heard the horn honking behind me, I glanced backward and saw an aggressive shuttle driver squeezing the bulb of his horn repeatedly and forcing his way slowly through the pedestrians.

I slowed, knowing that we had to time this just right. And Winnie shortened her steps to stay by my side.

Suddenly I doubled over.

My body tingled as the shuttle's grill passed through Winnie and me so that we were now within the clanking, rattletrap vehicle. The engine's pistons pounded up and down around me, and I spoke louder so Winnie could hear me.

"Walk faster now so we can stay inside the shuttle," I instructed her.

"Huh, so this is what a motor looks like when it's moving," she said from somewhere around the carburetor.

She and I quickened our stride so that the truck would mask us from the others. After fifty yards, I judged it safe to slow down again and let the shuttle go on. First the driver and then his passengers all gave little laughs as they felt us pass through them.

When the shuttle had gone, I risked a glance at the rear. The flags marking the front of the club were now about twenty yards behind us.

"Hurry up," I said, and we broke into a run.

A ripple of laughter ran through the dense crowd, marking our passage. But there were no shouts from Willamar to stay with the Fellowship.

"To the right," I said, and we headed into a side street, hiding in the doorway of a store. I peeked around the corner and saw the flags of the club march past us and toward the main gate on Scott Street.

We were free!

Chapter Four

You can't judge a treasure from the past by its price tag.
What we truly treasure of the past can take surprising forms—
like the Sphinx, odd machines, and buttered biscuits.

MISS DRAKE

We scooted through the turnstiles of the Fillmore
Street gate and headed
into the Joy Zone, the amusement area of the Exposition.

The Zone was mobbed
as it always was, and many
of the fairgoers must have
been first timers because
they had paused on the
broad avenue like Winnie
to stare. Each building's

front was shaped to show what was inside, so two giant ostrich statues welcomed one to the ostrich farm, and a titanic Sphinx and arch with hieroglyphics advertised the alligator farm, though the alligators most likely came from Florida, not Egypt. Towering above them all were redwood-size toy soldiers who stood guard before Toyland. Even though I had been here many times before, I felt as if I had wandered into the dream of some slumbering giant.

Around us, I heard English mainly, but I caught snatches of French and Spanish and Japanese and a dozen other languages too commenting on their extraordinary surroundings.

"The crowd's like a mini-UN," Winnie commented.

"Caleb used to say that we invited the world to our party, and the world came," I agreed proudly. "And with their exhibits, the people of the world shared their achievements, art, and lives with us."

Winnie pointed at the Scenic Railway with the artificial elephants holding up the track. "Hey, let's ride that."

I took her hand and gave a gentle tug. "No, I have something else in mind for your first ride."

Though the Zone's rides had been novel to a child of 1915, I was afraid that they would seem tame to a girl who was used to computerized, roboticized amusements of the twenty-first century.

But there was no way I could allow for the fair's chance delights. When I saw the float with the huge globe of the world bearing down on us, I drew Winnie to the side to give us a better view.

"What's wrong?" she asked.

"There's a parade coming," I said.

Like the Grand Bazaar of Istanbul, the Exposition had always provided wonderful chance encounters, bits of sweet serendipity. I hoped it would give Winnie meaningful memories just as it had Caleb.

Behind the float came hula dancers waving to the spectators, followed by Greeks in embroidered vests and red caps, Norwegian women with their hair in braids, Russians in fur capes, Maoris, and Chinese, each group doing a few steps of a dance. It was a preview for a folk dance festival later that afternoon.

When Caleb had encountered people from faraway places or wandered the state and national pavilions, his eyes had shone with all the excitement, wonder, and curiosity of a chick breaking out of its shell.

We joined the cheerful crowd trailing the dancers, and I glanced at Winnie, who danced a playful step or two. Though she was enjoying herself, this event wasn't a unique opportunity to her. After all, she only had to tap a few keys on her computer if she wanted to learn about the world, so the parade was simply a chance to party.

There was nothing wrong with having fun, but today needed to be extra special. So when we reached the Aeroscope, I slipped my arm around her shoulders and drew her toward the ride. "I want this to be your first taste of the Exposition."

A double-decker cabin was attached to a long metal structure 265 feet long of steel girders like a quarter-size Eiffel Tower lying on its side. At the very bottom was a 380-ton block of concrete serving as the counter-weight that with a motor would sling the cabin up into the air.

Winnie stared at it doubtfully. "Really? I think I'd rather see the alligators."

"Indulge me, please," I sniffed.

"All right, but you owe me," Winnie grumbled, and reluctantly tagged along as I climbed to the cabin's upper level.

Winnie gave a little cry and grabbed hold of me when the cabin lurched from the ground. The ride's engine coughed as it lifted the cabin higher and higher into the sky with the help of the counterweight. "Whoa!" she said as the sounds from the Zone, the boisterous barkers, and chattering pedestrians faded away. And then I could smell the bay and hear the gulls boasting as they glided alongside coasting on the winds.

Winnie gasped happily as the cabin swung in a slow circle in the sky, sinking and then rising again and again to give us another 360 degree view of the city, the bay and the fair. Below us, all 635 acres of the fair spread from east to west like a long, lovely Persian carpet of soft colors and elegant designs, lying alongside the brilliant blue bay to the north. Ornate ivory palaces glittered with bits of matching jewel-like colors—turquoise borders, orange and green domes, brilliant blue pools—within spacious courtyards full of fountains, art, and gardens.

I have been to many world fairs in the last couple of centuries, and there was none that could match the loveliness of San Francisco's. Though I had flown over the Exposition many times, it still took my breath away to see it from above. If the Council's rules for this excursion into the past hadn't specifically forbidden our true shapes, I would have taken Winnie for a flight like I used to do with Caleb.

As the ride ended and we returned to the earthly bustle, Winnie's comment was short and sweet. "Awesome," she said softly, grabbing my hand.

But she quickly let it go when we landed and scooted down the midway, now eager to sample more of it—whatever caught her eye next as we walked. She wouldn't budge until we rode on the Hippodrome Carousel, always one of my favorites. But I prodded her away from the replica of the Grand Canyon, and the mini Panama Canal rides that delighted fairgoers, promising I would take her to the real places instead.

There just wasn't time to see everything at the Zone if we also wanted to see some of the fair. But like Caleb, my energetic companion was curious about every astounding attraction. As I dashed after Winnie, I wished I had designed some magical leash for my pet.

Catching her by the shoulders, I warned her, "Settle down, or I'll take you to the Palace of Education and Social Economy." That threat always worked with Caleb, and it did with his descendant too!

Wrinkling her nose, Winnie was about to say something, when a man carrying a crate walked through her. The man chuckled, and the pup in the crate started barking loudly.

When Winnie jumped at the noise, I explained, "He must be heading to a dog show." I waved a hand. "The farm animals and pets were shown in a different part of the fair. Caleb won a red ribbon for his pet."

"What kind did he have?" Winnie asked curiously.

"A marmoset," I told her, smiling. "A hyperactive

monkey Caleb loved." I smiled, remembering how tiny Reggie would run around and around until he'd leap up on Caleb, climb inside his shirt, and fall asleep.

"Why didn't you tell me my great-granddad had a pet monkey?" Winnie asked in astonishment. I think he was beginning to sound more interesting to her after all.

"It didn't occur to me," I confessed, and tried to correct my error now. "Caleb liked anything with animals, the livestock exhibits, all the shows and competitions, everything with horses and camels. But I usually waited for him nearby. Some of the animals, especially the horses, acted strangely around me, sensing perhaps I was not what I seemed."

Winnie perked up at that. Since her mother, Liza, had worked in stables, horses seemed like cousins to her. "Let's see the horses."

"There's not enough time," I answered. "Besides, you'll see horses during your next riding class at school."

I tensed for the argument, but fortunately, Winnie was distracted by a laughing woman with large, lively eyes surrounded by reporters and photographers. "Oh, look at her!"

"That's Mabel Normand, the actress," I murmured to Winnie, who looked blank. "She was a big star in silent films. A lot of celebrities came to the fair."

"Would I know any of them?" Winnie asked.

"Probably not." I was used to having the famous people of one generation become unknown to the next—and in Winnie's case, it was several generations later. "But you might recognize who she is wearing."

Miss Normand strutted past, wearing a jaunty hat and what looked like a white fox stole draped around her neck. Just then the fox snapped at a pesky fly circling his tail.

Winnie squinted. "Is that Reynard?"

"That's what Reynard looks like when he's smitten," I chuckled. "He took quite a fancy to Miss Normand and would turn himself into whatever color she needed to match her outfits. She wore him everywhere."

"Oh, how funny he looks," said Winnie.

"Foolish is more like it," I sniffed. "It nearly broke his heart when she cast him aside for a family of minks, so don't mention her to him."

A plump, dignified gentleman gazed at Miss Normand, then pulled a large watch out of his vest pocket. I peeked over his shoulder so I could set my dainty gold wristwatch to 1915 time.

I clicked my tongue in disappointment. "Too bad. We've missed the mine explosion in the Palace of Mines and Metallurgy. Caleb always enjoyed watching the rescue, but there's something else you might like."

A major goal of the fair had been to show off the latest technologies, but what had been new and unique in 1915 had become old and commonplace by Winnie's time. Many of the things that had fascinated Caleb like baby incubators and the transcontinental telephone calls would make his great-granddaughter yawn. So I'd narrowed down my choices to just a few.

"Let's start at the Palace of Transportation," I said.

"Will they have flying carpets there?" Winnie asked eagerly as we left the Zone.

"No, you'll stay firmly on the ground." I led her to Henry Ford's automobile Assembly Line. "Normals created it, but even magicals used to think it was incredible."

Once inside, Winnie pushed her way through the crowd to the front ropes. A skeletal car chassis, like the metal frame of a bed with tires, began to move along a track. When it passed through different stations, workers added parts like the engine, the black sides, the doors, headlights, and windshield. Soon a complete Model T Ford rolled out the doorway ready to be shipped to a car dealer to be sold.

As we strolled away from the palace, Winnie admitted, "Well, that was cool. A car in . . . ?"

I checked my watch. "Ten minutes. Caleb thought it was 'cool' too." Though the word he had used was *jim-dandy.* "He never grew tired of watching cars being assembled, and when he grew up, he always bought Fords. He even gave Amelia a red Mustang for her thirtieth birthday. We made a lot of happy memories scooting around in her Jezebel."

Just then I saw Willamar's flags advancing slowly toward us. I'd made an error when I'd anticipated his itinerary.

"Come along." Seizing Winnie's hand, I tugged her into a small enclosed courtyard.

"Phew," said Winnie. "It stinks here." I looked around and saw we shared the courtyard with a dozen men in suits and bowler hats, smoking cigars.

I wrinkled my nose in agreement, but a hundred years ago, tobacco was quite popular among normals because they didn't know how poisonous it was. I've always believed that if normals were meant to produce smoke, they would have been born with two stomachs and able to breathe fire on their own, like us dragons.

Still, as unhealthy as the cigar smoke was, I smiled recalling my smoke-shaping contests with Sebastian, Caleb's father and Winnie's great-great-grandfather. Of course, the wispy circles he blew were no match for my triangles, squares—and even once a pentagon. He didn't mind losing, though, grinning like a small boy while my hazy creations floated around his head.

But the smoky stench was making my pet gasp. "We

need to stay out of the war in Europe," a man with a white mustache said.

As the others nodded sagely, Winnie asked, "What war are they talking about?"

"World War One," I said. Feeling sad, I suddenly wanted to get away from remembering the war and the sorrow it caused for all sides.

So I peeked around the entrance and saw the last flag of Willamar's club moving away, and by mutual agreement, we broke into a run in the opposite direction to breathe the fresh air from the bay again.

CHAPTER FIVE

Humans create their magic with their hearts
rather than with wands, and trouble with
their mouths rather than their minds.

MISS DRAKE

All the pathways linking the palaces and courtyards were covered in pink sand. As she jogged alongside me, Winnie stooped and scooped up some, but of course, her hand passed right through the sand.

"Rats," she said. "This colored stuff would be great in an art project."

"The sand isn't dyed," I told her. "It comes from

Monterey about a hundred and twenty miles away. It was toasted to bring out the color. The pink sand sets off the cream-colored buildings perfectly," I added. "If I had known I'd have such an artistic friend in the future, I'd have saved the piles of sand that always stowed away in my shoes."

Keeping a watchful eye for our friends from the twenty-first century, we dipped into some of the other palaces that I hoped might interest her. But I'd guessed wrong, and she walked through them, bored.

When my failures mounted, I headed to the Palace of Liberal Arts to something that I was sure would tickle her fancy. But when Winnie saw the giant candlestick-shaped telephone with the sofa at its base, she simply said, "Weird."

I studied it, deciding that it would seem like a bizarre piece of furniture to a girl used to cell phones. I was beginning to think we should return to the Zone, but when I looked down to ask her, Winnie was gone.

"Winnie!" I called over and over as I hunted frantically up and down the aisles. Much to my surprise, I found her standing in front of an enormous fourteen-ton typewriter that was thrice as tall as anyone in the room.

Thump. Thump. Thump. The huge keys struck a sheet of paper nine feet wide, printing the news of the day in huge letters.

The rhythmic drumming had drawn Winnie, and I laughed to see my friend of the computer age captivated by the workings of such an old-fashioned machine.

"I've only seen typewriters in photos," she told me when I joined her.

Winnie was used to tapping effortlessly on keyboards, not this noisy, clumsy device. "It's like meeting a dinosaur," I said with a grin.

She smiled back at me. "Or a dragon."

I led Winnie outside the Palace of Liberal Arts, through the door that faced the Tower of Jewels.

"Look up," I commanded Winnie, and she gasped. It was late afternoon, but the sun was still making a dazzling display on the cut glass gems above us.

Hanging on the sides of the tallest building in the fair, over four hundred feet high, were more than a hundred thousand cut-glass gems—dangling, dancing, and sparkling white, pink, yellow, purple, and red in the sunlight. Each round jewel a miniature living star and collectively a galaxy that took my breath away with their glory and beauty as they seemed to flash in time to a spritely march a nearby band was playing.

"Yikes," she said. "Look at all the Novagems. Bet Willamar would love to be able to take those home."

I chuckled, knowing he had probably wished the same thing today.

We were near the main entrance to the fair, and everywhere there were things to see. Crowds were pouring through the Scott Street turnstiles, looking happy and ready for a good time. Small children were splashing the water in a large round pool, and Winnie ran up captivated by the statues of sea creatures in the center of the fountain—the lithe mermaids and stately sea horses—walking happily around it so she could see them all.

The delightful concert stopped, and audience and uniformed musicians began to pass by. Winnie's attention, though, was all on the creatures in the fountain. "They're like figures on a carousel," she said. "I'd like to ride a sea horse."

"Perhaps one day," I told her, imagining an outing to the South Seas, where one of my acquaintances might oblige a smaller-size rider.

Winnie twisted her head around to look at me. "When is 'one day'?"

I waved for her to step to the side. "Winnie! Get out of the way!"

Too late. A dignified bearded man in his sixties wearing a dashing military cap and ornate red jacket walked through her. Neither was in any danger of broken bones, but it seemed, well, disrespectful to tickle such a great man and make him burst into a loud laugh that trailed behind him as he continued striding.

I gave a deep, mortified sigh. "Well, I don't think any of our companions can brag they literally bumped into John Philip Sousa."

"Who?" she asked as she stared at the retreating composer and conductor.

"You may not know the name, but you'll recognize his music." I hummed "The Stars and Stripes Forever."

She nodded in time to the song. "Yeah, I've heard that. So he wrote it, huh?"

"Yes, and many other stirring marches bands will still play a hundred years from now," I said as we entered a broad courtyard where tall columns encircled us.

For a moment, I felt as if I were once again strolling through St. Peter's piazza in Rome—except there, the pillars hadn't been topped by twinkling star maidens.

The Exposition often reminded me of my travels because so many of its structures were inspired by ancient ones—the Oregon State Building was even modeled on Athens's Parthenon but used towering redwoods instead of marble. Sometimes the fair seemed like my enormous charm bracelet, full of souvenirs from my journeys.

Fourteen flags waved a hundred feet above our heads, and at the base of each flagpole, gentle-faced elephants stood on watch. Winnie stood on tiptoes, trying to stroke the trunk of one.

"I feel like I've seen him before," she said.

"You have," I told her, pleased she had recalled it. "Remember when we took the ferry to Sausalito to get your school materials? The pole bearer here became a whimsical lamppost by the boat pier!"

"Whaddya know?" Winnie said, and as she smiled at the elephant above her, a musician in black tie and tails waddled by with a bass in a canvas covering. If the orchestra was gathering, Lady Gravelston's ball was about to start soon. "Come. I want to show you my favorite place before dark."

Among the fairgoers on the long east-west avenues, we began to see men in top hats and women in gowns and glittering with jewelry. Other formally attired men and women rode in rented wicker carts powered by electric batteries. These well-dressed folk would have been the guests invited to meet Lady Gravelston.

Her grandfather had looted the Heart of Kubera from the Summer Palace fifty-five years ago when the British invaded China. And the Manchus, who ruled China then, had taken it in turn as part of their spoils when they conquered Tibet 140 years before the British attack. Some might call them victors, others plunderers.

Tonight Lady Gravelston would wear this much-sought-after prize. The local newspapers had covered the plans for the ball for days and printed elaborate drawings of Lady Gravelston's jewelry. An army of police had surrounded the California Building, where the ball was being held—which had made the gem's disappearance all the more remarkable.

We left the road when we reached a lagoon. Beyond it lay the gracefully shaped Palace of Fine Arts. Inside the long windowless building were modern paintings and drawings, and breathtaking sculpture from all over the world. But to me and many others, the true treasure was outside—a beautiful domed structure, a giant rotunda, and a line of tall colonnades that curved around it, facing the lagoon that welcomed all to stop and rest in a place of serenity.

Winnie put a hand on her stomach. "All this walking is making me hungry again."

"Ah, great minds think alike," I said, stopping near a sweet grouping of statues, a circle of children dancing merrily around a tall spray of water. We could see the palace's elegant dome in the background and a pair of curious swans rippling their path toward us. I sat daintily on the grass and motioned to Winnie, who plopped beside me.

"I always make sure my jackets have deep pockets," I told her as I unloaded a pile of scones and rose cakes and laid them between us on a large linen handkerchief.

Winnie was impressed, taking off her gloves and reaching for a rose cake.

"You swiped all of this?" she asked. "No one stopped you?"

"And no one was turned into a toad or dung beetle either," I said firmly, ending the conversation so we could enjoy our tasty repast by the water.

I smiled, remembering how Caleb would bring me scones from a palace displaying food just across the way, the "Palace of Nibbling Arts" as some folk named it. We'd eat them here too, tossing our leftover bits and crumbs to the waiting birds on the lagoon.

After Winnie finished her third pastry, I tried to sound casual as I asked, "So what do you think of the Exposition?"

"Well," she said, pausing to lick her fingers. "It's kind of like the biggest toy box ever."

I was speechless with disappointment. It was like saying my beautiful scales were the same as the sequins on a doll dress. Was my pet blind to charm, beauty, and wonder? Had her modern world come to this? Comparing everything to a toy box!

But I could see she was working something out in her head, so I held my tongue while her mind sorted her thoughts.

"I mean, you gotta dig around, but there's fun stuff," she finally said.

"Yes, I suppose we could return to the Zone," I said resignedly.

"No, it's not just the Zone that's fun. The fair has a lot of stuff to look at and a lot of stuff that makes you think," she said quickly, her tongue trying to keep up with her thoughts. "And it's not just the exhibits that do that. It's the buildings themselves and all the people. And it's the dancing and the music. And . . . and it's the ideas. There's so many of 'em here!" She stopped to gasp for air and then started again but now with awe in her voice. "The world's such a big place, isn't it? And it's stuffed with so many fabulous things!"

I was beginning to understand and this time with pleasure. "Ah, so that's what you mean by your toy box."

She put her hands on her knees, and her voice rose with excitement. "And we normals may not look or dress or talk like one another, but we're all the same inside. It's like when we went up in the Aeroscope, and all the different buildings became part of something bigger and more wonderful. We normals can be part of something bigger and better as well."

Caleb's encounters here had made him realize the same things as Winnie, and he'd blossomed into a kinder, more thoughtful and appreciative man. Who knew what she'd become with a little encouragement from me? Training humans isn't about making them obedient and spiritless; it's about developing the best in them.

A lump caught in my throat. I was glad we had come. "Yes, that's the real fair."

When she didn't respond right away, I glanced at her and saw her wistful expression.

"Oh, I wish my dad could be here." Her hand brushed the air. "He would have loved what the sun does to the palaces right now. It sort of dances on the windows and the walls. He'd never want to leave the fair. I can just picture him running from one building to another, wanting to see everything and wanting me to see it with him. It's our Jewel City."

"Sparkling by the bay," I agreed.

Then she was silent, and so was I. In the growing twilight, we watched the swans sail off, floating across the lagoon. I was flabbergasted . . . and delighted. Whenever Winnie spoke of her father, it was with love, and I could see how the fair sparked her memory of him . . . just as it did my affection for Caleb. My pet had more understanding and more heart than I had given her credit.

As dusk drifted into night, the globed streetlights came on, their reflections glimmering on the water. Winnie roused from her thoughts. "Is it time to see Great-Grandad Caleb yet?"

From a distance came the faint strains of a waltz. The ball for Lady Gravelston had begun, and the club would be there watching.

"Not quite," I said, getting up and brushing bits of grass from my skirt. "So we have time to see the light show first. Let's find a good spot."

When Winnie joined me, I noticed she had stuffed her gloves into the pocket of her jacket. Good thing no one could see us. We walked to the Tower of Jewels and turned toward the North Gardens.

"Ooh," said Winnie. "Look at the Tower now. It's glowing."

No lights were visible anywhere, but hidden lamps flooded the pale-colored walls and tower. In this light, the jewels lost their sparkle but framed the Tower with a ghostly shimmer. The Exposition at night had an enchantment all its own.

"I bet you magicals helped light up the fair," said Winnie.

"Not at all," I corrected her. "All this was done by human minds with human hands."

"Really?" Winnie spread her arms out like she wanted to hug everything and then twirled in a circle. "So we made all this?"

It's what I loved about normals. "Sometimes all you need is enough ingenuity—and some money as well—to make a brilliant and amazing place."

We found a spot among the crowds gathering on the long green lawns of the North Gardens. Before us spread the inky waters of the bay.

Even though the air was brisk, all the warm bodies close kept us snug. Winnie even unbuttoned her jacket.

Boom!

As if the gun had woken them up, pipes as tall as flagpoles began hissing like nests of snakes, spraying vapor into the air from nozzles all along their lengths. A stationary pastel-painted locomotive chugged into life, adding jets of steam to the fine mist that began to stretch like a giant fan across the bay and high into the heavens.

Then, from an artificial castle offshore, two banks of

forty-eight large spotlights splashed their colored beams across the cloud as if it were an ever-changing canvas. The hues danced like an aurora borealis over the bay, blending at times and then drifting apart again only to spread outward in rainbow plumes, the colored light painting flags of nations or a parade of marching monsters. They called it a fireless fireworks show of steam and spotlights.

With one voice, the crowd oohed and aahed. Winnie's up-turned face was full of astonishment too.

Then, as the pipes and locomotive stopped spraying steam and the mist dissipated, the spotlights were turned off. In the darkness, we heard the drone of a biplane engine drawing closer like a giant bumblebee.

"Look over there." I nodded toward thin bright trails rising through the dark sky, made by sparking flares attached to the tips of the airplane's canvas wings. The engine changed pitch as the plane nosed down and then up again in a flaming circle. Then the pilot repeated the process in a series of loops that looked like a ribbon of fire twirling through the night. It was as close as any normal could come to flying like a fire-breathing dragon.

Winnie stood up to see better, laughing in delight.

"It's a young stunt pilot named Art Smith," I told her, "doing tricks in his biplane."

"Wow!" she shouted as the crowd cheered stunt after stunt till he disappeared into the darkness. "That was great."

I felt like a magician who had pulled her last rabbit out of her hat. And yet, there was still one last and best reveal for Winnie: Caleb.

It was time to find him now . . . and I knew exactly where to look.

Chapter Six

*When you travel to the past, make sure you get
a roundtrip ticket.*

∽ MISS DRAKE ∽

Now that the light show was over, some people had begun to leave the Exposition. There weren't many, though—perhaps because it was a Saturday night, and they knew they could sleep late tomorrow.

I used the Tower of Jewels as a landmark to guide us to the right spot and kept Winnie moving when she was inclined to dawdle. We didn't stop until we reached one of the kiosks dotting the ground. It was a cylindrical building about twelve feet in diameter, and from the ground to the finial decorating the domed roof, it was about twenty feet high. Windows with curving tops had been cut all around its sides.

The Zone was the place to go to select a memento, but this one was a pack rat's nest of souvenir spoons, dishes, paperweights, postcards, buttons with landmarks, jars of candy and licorice, as well as toy racing cars and airplanes on the window counters and on the shelves inside. In fact, the owner reminded me of a rat the way he looked around nervously as if he expected a cat to jump on him at any moment.

If this island of commerce seemed out of place on the broad avenue of artfully placed trees, fountains, and statues holding glittering jewels, the customers didn't seem to care. They wanted a little something that would remind them years later of a wonderful afternoon. After a few centuries of travel, of course, I'd learned to fight that impulse. If I hadn't, I would be living on a mountain of knickknacks by now.

Instead, I tried to fix the sights and sounds of each day in my memory. When I had first met Winnie, she had expected me to have a hoard of gold, but what I treasured was a hoard of memories.

Even the feeding frenzy at the kiosk would become another one. The kiosk drew everyone—from the well-dressed families to one scruffy-looking sailor I spotted heading for its wares. Used to walking on a swaying ship's deck, his gait was a dead giveaway that he was an old salt.

Winnie craned her neck as she examined the crowd. "Is Great-Granddad here?"

I glanced at my wristwatch. It was a half hour to the theft of the Heart of Kubera. My past self had arrived here with Caleb just before the thief struck, though I wasn't sure about the precise minute.

"Not yet," I said, "but you'll be able to see him soon."

"You said I'd be able to meet him." Bored, she waved her arm through a statue's pedestal. "But how can I if he won't be able to see me?"

"I meant you'd meet him in the general sense," I said. "At the time, I didn't know what kind of enchantment we'd use."

"In the meantime, I might as well check on what's here," Winnie said, and stepped right into the crowd. I heard the giggling as she moved through people to the kiosk itself.

It was on the tip of my tongue to call and retrieve her, but I reasoned Lady Louhi's spell would prevent her from interacting with anyone from the past—apart from the tickling, and that simply made a happy experience a tad happier.

A man in heavy work shoes stood by the counter with a little girl of eight in a clean but patched dress. She stood on tiptoe to point at something hanging in the rear of the stall. "I want the monkey puppet."

The man's face fell when he saw the price. "I'm afraid not."

Winnie's head appeared from the man's side, and the man squirmed and chuckled. She was becoming a little too comfortable popping in and out of people. "Ooh, the puppet's neat. I hope Great-Granddad bought it."

I stared up at the glass dome of the Palace of Horticulture, glowing green from within and thought a moment. "I don't remember him buying it tonight, but he bought a lot of little things throughout the year. It would have been easy for me to forget."

"Well, did you see him put one in his time capsule?" Winnie asked.

"No, he did that by himself," I said. "He was reaching that age when he needed some privacy."

"I bet a nosy dragon like you didn't like that," she said with a grin, and then disappeared into the crowd.

No, I hadn't, but it was a stage that all my pets go through. With a little luck and a lot of coaching from me, they emerged at the end of the stage once again as acceptable company.

While Winnie browsed, I kept one eye on the stall

and one eye on the avenue. Idly, I watched the sailor take his hand from his coat pocket and sift through a basket of wooden whistles on the counter. A little hand-lettered sign said:

THIS BASKET ONLY
One whistle for 10¢
Two for 15¢

"See anything you like?" asked Mr. Ratty, the stall keeper.

The sailor looked at the outside of the kiosk, where buttons with landmarks hung on a long cardboard strip. He took one with the Tower of Jewels. "I'll get this one."

He offered a coin on his palm. Instead of picking it up with his fingers, Mr. Ratty's hand covered the sailor's. When the sailor lifted his hand away, his fingers were curled around something that he quickly hid in his coat pocket. What had Mr. Ratty passed to the sailor? A roll of money?

While Mr. Ratty and the sailor were taking care of business, the little girl had noticed the basket and begun to sift through it.

Mr. Ratty made shooing motions with his hand. "You don't want those, little girl. Some of them are defective."

As he stretched to take the entire basket, a lady

grabbed his wrist. "Hey, mister, you got any spoons with the Palace of Fine Arts?"

She was a woman of medium height, but the coils of her gray hair lay flat on her head like a woven rag rug.

Mr. Ratty flashed his teeth. "I'll be with you in a minute, ma'am."

"I'm late to meet my husband," the woman said, keeping her grip on him.

"Uh, well, let me see," Mr. Ratty said, distracted.

At that moment, I saw a tall, blond woman in her thirties, head held up high on a long, swan-like neck despite the weight of a waterfall of curls under her smart, little straw hat. The 1915 version of me strode along confidently—like other "New Women" of that era as we marched for the right to vote and equal education and opportunities with the men.

The eleven-year-old boy did more than keep up with my long stride. Black hair flying, gray eyes sparkling, he was a bundle of vitality—sometimes he ran alongside me, sometimes behind and sometimes in front. Dear, dear Caleb. He had enough energy to power all of San Francisco and a smile to light up the state.

In three years, that would change when his parents died in the Spanish flu epidemic, like so many others around the world. After that tragic event, he rarely smiled or laughed, and he threw all his immense energy first into his studies and then into his work, charities, and family. As an adult, he had tried his best to make this imperfect world a better one.

It was this boy, though, that I had come to see once again and add new details to my hoard of memories. And it was this boy I wanted Winnie to know.

The 1915 me would have kept walking along the avenue. Caleb, though, suddenly veered toward the stall. "Let's see what they've got, Miss Drake."

When I heard him call my name, I almost answered him and felt a pang when I realized he was talking to the 1915 version of me trudging after him. "Your mother's going to blame me for keeping you out late."

Caleb grinned at the 1915 me. "I'll get around her. I always do." He spoke with the confidence of a child who knew he was loved and treasured.

I almost reached to try to touch his cheek, but at that moment, Winnie appeared from a giggling woman. "So that's Great-Granddad?"

"Yes," I said wistfully, not taking my eyes off him. We were about to witness Caleb in one of his finer moments—one I had brought Winnie all the way through time and space to see.

In her typically irreverent way, Winnie examined him

from all sides as he inspected the souvenirs. "You sure? I don't see the family resemblance."

I waved a hand vaguely. "It's the ears."

Winnie pressed a hand against her right ear, flattening it against her head. "Mine don't stick out that much."

With my finger, I sketched the curve of their ears in the air. "No, but they're shaped the same. Now hush and pay attention."

Just then, the girl took a five-inch-long whistle from the basket. Painted on its side was a little red hen. "I want this, Papa."

Her father dug in his pockets and then sighed heavily. It was clear the whistles were also too expensive. "You don't want those, honey. The man says it could be broken."

The little girl blew a shrill note on the whistle. "See? It's all right."

The man's face sagged into a sad, hopeless expression.

Caleb was at his most impetuous when he was being kind. He didn't see why he couldn't love and indulge others just as his parents loved and indulged him.

"Let me buy it for you," Caleb offered.

The girl shrank against her father's leg. "We don't take charity from strangers," her father said with great dignity.

Caleb bent over, so he was eye level with the little girl. "My name's Caleb. What's yours?"

She spoke barely above a whisper. "Lily."

Caleb straightened. "You see? I'm not a stranger now. Let's play a song together." He reached blindly into the basket and picked the first whistle that came to hand.

It was paler than the others, either a different wood or possibly some other material. Could it be ivory? *Not at that price,* I thought. The whistle was a little longer than Lily's, about six inches in length. A line of holes was neatly carved on the top, and as Caleb spun around, I could see a well-crafted and graceful etching of a leaping mongoose on the side.

Setting it to his lips, he blew a series of notes, his fingers dancing over the air holes. Beaming, Lily answered him with a few off-key notes of her own.

"Huh, so that's Great-Granddad." Winnie nodded approvingly. "Nice guy."

"He is." I corrected myself quickly, "I mean, was."

Good-bye, dear Caleb. I tried to keep savoring this moment and not think about the great sorrows that waited for him.

"You look sad," Winnie observed.

"It's one of the side effects of time travel." I put my hand on her shoulder. Every pet grows up to be someone unique, but it wouldn't be such a bad thing if Winnie became a little like her great-grandfather. "I'll tell you what he did, and you can judge just how nice he . . . uh . . . was."

"And that woman's you?" When I nodded, Winnie observed, "You were a lot prettier then."

Apparently, the Spriggs Academy was teaching Winnie everything but tact. "I was in my Lucrezia Borgia phase at the time, and now I am not. So shush."

Lily's father stroked her hair as his daughter looked up at him hopefully. Then he nodded to Caleb. "Thank you."

Even though he was in the middle of waiting on the Spoon Woman, Mr. Ratty turned when he heard Caleb and Lily's attempts at music. "That whistle's not for sale, sonny."

Caleb set a dime and a nickel on the counter, paying for both whistles. "But it was in the basket."

"That one in your hand's already spoken for." Mr. Ratty thrust his palm toward the boy. "Give it to me."

As a New Woman, the 1915 me wasn't going to tolerate male arrogance—either to her or her pet. "Then the whistle should not have been in the basket for someone to find it."

"It was a mistake, Miss," Mr. Ratty protested.

"Then you must live with the consequences of your

error," the 1915 me informed him, "as we all must." Nodding to Lily and Lily's father, she took Caleb's hand. "Come, Caleb."

"No, wait! You can't!" Knocking paperweights off the counter, Mr. Ratty began to climb through a window to follow them, but the Spoon Woman shoved him inside the kiosk.

"Where do you think you're going?" she demanded. "You're still waiting on me."

"I'll be with you in a moment," Mr. Ratty said. He pushed her away and pulled himself through the window.

His feet had no sooner dropped on the ground outside his stall, when Lily's father blocked his way. "You leave the boy be."

"But he's got my whistle." Mr. Ratty tried to slide around Lily's father, but Lily herself kicked his shin.

"It's his whistle now," she said.

When Mr. Ratty yelped in pain, I glimpsed what looked like a tan streak of lightning darting in and out through the forest of people's legs. I would have sworn it was a mouse, and yet no mouse could move that fast.

Right then, Winnie wriggled her shoulders. "Hey, stop tickling me."

"Don't exaggerate," I told her. But when I looked at

her, I saw that my hand had dropped down below her still moving shoulders and *into* her body.

Something was very wrong! While I was still out of phase and protected, Winnie was not. She was truly in 1915 and visible to all!

I cursed myself for a fool. I had been so busy paying attention to a past pet that I had failed the most basic duty: to protect my present one.

"We have to go," I said urgently, but of course, she could no longer hear me. And when I pulled at her arm, she couldn't feel me.

As I desperately tried to think of a way to get her away from here, a woman cried in an accented voice that rang along the avenue. "T"ief! Purse snatcher!"

At the same moment, the Spoon Woman whipped around. She looked down at the empty space at her feet and then at her large black bag on the ground by Winnie. Her arm whipped up, and she aimed her finger at Winnie like the barrel of a pistol.

"What're you doing with my purse?" she demanded angrily.

CHAPTER SEVEN

Time travelers shouldn't change the past any more than
leopards should change their spots.

Winnie

"You can see me?" I gasped in amazement.

"Of course, I can." The Spoon Woman pointed at the ugly old bag by my feet, "and I can see my purse too!"

What I saw was my ring on my gloveless hand. It was flashing *red . . . red . . . red. . . .* I didn't like the look of that. But I already felt I was in danger.

Had my charm stopped working? I put a hand

up to my badge but it was gone. I looked down to see where I had dropped it.

"Police!" the Spoon Woman hollered, and lunged at me before I could find anything.

I got a second shock when I felt her hand grab the collar of my jacket. I was not only visible, but I was touchable too.

"Help!" I looked around frantically for Miss Drake. Though she was probably right by me, she was still invisible and in ghost mode.

"Police!" When the Spoon Woman yelled again, people began to stop and stare.

"I didn't take your purse," I insisted, tapping my toe against the bag. "I don't know how it got here."

"Says you," the Spoon Woman snarled. "You're caught, and you're caught good. It's jail for you, girlie." And she gave me a shake.

"Hey, don't hurt her," Great-Granddad Caleb said. It was funny calling this boy Great-Granddad. "You got your purse, so why don't you let her go?"

The Spoon Woman used her free hand to shove him. "Get lost, kiddo."

Great-Granddad staggered a few yards and then fell down, but he got up and started toward me again. "I said to leave her alone!"

When I saw the Spoon Woman ball her free hand into a fist and pull her arm back for a wicked punch, I tried to warn him, "No, stop."

When he kept right on coming to my rescue, I was sorry I'd gotten water on his portrait now, and who cared if his ears stuck out? I didn't want him getting hurt for my sake. I had to do something to distract the Spoon Woman.

So I bit her . . . hard.

Her coat sleeve tasted of nasty strong soap, so I guess we both got our punishments.

"Yow!" she howled, but she kept her grip on me.

Great-Grandpa had a determined look on his face as he reached for her wrist to yank it away from me.

"No," I tried to say through a mouthful of wool.

"Release—" he began to say when he suddenly vanished.

The Spoon Woman turned her head this way and that. "What? Where'd the brat go?"

When I saw people in the crowd stagger to the side and look around puzzled, I figured that Great-Granddad's Miss Drake had cast an invisibility spell on herself and him so she could carry him away from the fight.

If only his Miss Drake had enchanted me too.

At the same time, the mean stall keeper dropped to

his knees at the feet of Lily and her father. "My whistle!" he wailed.

I knew if I gave her enough time, my Miss Drake would save me. But first I had to get loose from Spoon Woman. But how?

When the Spoon Woman had shaken me, my unbuttoned jacket had felt a little looser around my neck. I wondered if I could slip from it.

Bending my knees, I shot my arms straight up. My jacket's sleeves slid right off me, leaving the Spoon Woman holding my jacket like I'd just shed my outer skin. I sprang away like a rabbit before she could grab me again.

A man tried to nab me, but my forearm knocked his hand away. A woman stretched toward me, but I ducked under her fingers.

Behind me, I heard the Spoon Woman go, "Oof! Get out of my way, Clumsy!" she said angrily to someone. I wondered what kind person had blocked her.

What I wouldn't give for my old running shoes right now. And while I was wishing, how about jeans instead of a frilly skirt and petticoat? As I ran, my big floppy hat flew off my head. Good riddance!

Despite my clothing, I could have gotten away quickly on a straight course with no obstacles, but I had to keep weaving through and around the mob.

"You're not getting away from me, you little thief!" the Spoon Woman puffed. It sounded like she was gaining on me.

I raced blind around the corner of a building, and I bumped into something soft. I bounced off and onto the ground. As I lay there, a short, middle-aged woman looked down at me. Her long wool coat was open so I could see she was wearing a green striped blouse with a cameo fastened to the collar. "Are you all right?"

I could hear the Spoon Woman shouting from close by, "Stop, thief!"

I jumped to my feet and was going to take off, but the cameo woman grabbed my arm and I couldn't break her grip. There was real muscle underneath all her softness. "Did you take something? Mind you, don't try to lie to me."

"No." I shook my head. "It's all a frame-up."

She didn't look at me long, but she looked at me hard like she was trying to read my mind. "I've taught a little bit and I've known a lot of children, so I can recognize when a child's fibbing and when she's telling the truth. Crouch down behind that statue."

I squatted behind the tall pedestal of a pioneer woman and her children, barely a few seconds before the Spoon Woman came panting along.

"Have you seen a weaselly little girl running by?" the Spoon Woman demanded.

"No," the cameo woman said. "I can truthfully say that I have not seen anyone of that description."

"I'll catch her, and when I do, that little thief is going to jail," the Spoon Woman promised.

A few minutes later, the cameo woman said, "She's gone. You're safe."

"Thanks for covering up for me," I said when I stood up. When she drew her eyebrows together as if puzzled, I added, "You know. Lying for me?"

"I didn't lie," the cameo woman assured me. "You don't look like any weasel I've met. But what did that disagreeable woman say you stole?"

"A big black bag," I said.

The cameo woman nodded, satisfied. "Which she had in her hand." She folded her arms to study me. "Frame-up. Covering up. You don't talk like any girl I know. Where do you come from, child?"

I tried to figure how to answer her. Technically, I lived only a mile or two away, but time wise, it was a hundred years. "My home's . . . uh . . . faraway." That was sort of true. "I came with a friend, but she must've gotten lost."

"Well, I'll stay with you until you get together again." The woman patted my arm. "I came with my daughter, and now I can't find her either." She added proudly, "Rose's a crackerjack reporter for the *San Francisco*

Bulletin, so she's always stopping to chat with someone here and there to get a story. When she turns up, she'll know how to locate your friend."

When my mom and me were on the run from my granddad, I'd learned not to say much to strangers. And even though this woman had just saved me from jail, I didn't want her asking awkward questions. I guess she thought I was being shy because she began chatting to make me feel more comfortable.

I heard all about her train ride from her Missouri farm, and then her round face started to glow when she told me about taking a boat ride on the bay at night and seeing the shining Exposition, and behind it the lights of San Francisco on the hills, twinkling higher and higher. "I tell you, I didn't know where the lights stopped and the stars began."

I realized then that even though we had experienced San Francisco a hundred years apart, we felt the same wonder about this place.

"And then yesterday I waded in the Pacific Ocean." She tapped her shoe on the ground as if she were dipping her toe into the sea. "Fancy that, me in all that water. It was wonderful. I do love the ocean so much."

I grinned, relaxing at last. "Me too," I said, putting out my hand. "My name's Winifred Burton."

"What a lovely name." She took my hand and shook it. "My name's Laura Ingalls Wilder."

It took a moment for the name to click inside my head, and when it did, I stopped breathing. This was a dream come true.

"You can . . . um . . . let go of my hand, Winifred," she said.

But I was too stunned and kept on holding onto her. "Not *the* Laura Ingalls Wilder. You're my *favorite* author."

Mrs. Wilder looked confused. "No, no, my daughter, Rose, is the author. Rose Wilder Lane, you must have heard of her. I just write a little column about raising chickens and such for the *Missouri Ruralist* back home."

I thought about every time-travel movie I'd seen. Say the wrong thing and there'd be no Little House books to read. Or say the right thing and there would be. I flipped a coin inside my head and took a chance. "You should tell people about when you were a kid."

"Aren't you a caution?" She flapped a hand at me. "Now you sound just like my daughter."

"I bet you got lotsa stories. You could fill up whole books. And . . . and . . . uh . . ." My voice trailed off. How far should I go? Or had I gone far enough?

"Books, is it now? That's a good one, all right. . . ." Her voice trailed off too, like something was tickling the back of her brain. "I intend to try to do some writing that will count. . . . That's my dream. Can you read my mind, Winifred?"

It's funny how maybe everyone at the fair thought Mabel Normand was famous, while no one knew who Laura Ingalls Wilder was. And yet by my time they'd switch places. "I can guarantee you that's the best dream."

Her eyes twinkled at me. "Oh, so now you're a fortune-teller from the Joy Zone."

Before I could encourage her any further, a familiar voice trumpeted in my ear. "Well, there you are, Winifred." Miss Drake set her hand on my shoulder. She gave it a firm squeeze, which I figured was a warning to shut up.

I was glad to see her but also sorry that she had butted in. "Oh, Miss Drake. I'd like to introduce you to Mrs. Laura Ingalls Wilder."

"Charmed, I'm sure," Miss Drake said, shaking her hand politely. "I know your daughter's work. I believe I saw her a few minutes ago near the bandstand interviewing Henry Ford."

Mrs. Wilder spread her arms. "Now that you two are reunited. I think I'll head that way and track down my wandering Rose. Good-bye, Winifred."

As she walked off, I couldn't help myself. "Remember,

write books about when you were a kid," I called. "Me and my friends'll read 'em all, I promise."

She stopped and looked over her shoulder at me. "If you aren't the strangest child." But then she laughed. "Well, it's one thing when Rose prods me, but now you too. Who knows what the future has in store? Books, oh, my!" And with a wave, she disappeared into the crowd.

Miss Drake pulled me in the opposite direction. "You weren't supposed to tamper with the past, Winifred Burton."

When she used my full name, I knew she must be angry. "You heard her," I argued. "I was just helping history along."

"Leave it to you to start a time paradox," she hissed in exasperation. "It will serve you right if her books are missing from your bookshelf when we get home. And it will tick off the Council to have to fix a mess you made."

That would be awful, but it was too late now. "How come Mrs. Wilder could see you?" I asked.

Miss Drake let go of me to point at her collar. "I took off my charm and hid it."

"Okay, well, why didn't you warn me that I was going to get into trouble at the kiosk?" I asked.

Miss Drake dropped her arm. "I recall there was an attempted purse snatching, but I was too busy casting an invisibility spell on Caleb and myself. And anyway, even if I had looked at the suspect, I wouldn't have recognized you because we hadn't met yet."

"I thought you weren't supposed to do magic in public where humans could see you," I said.

"We're not, but it was either that or rip that horrid woman's head off," Miss Drake explained. "I assumed— quite rightly—that all eyes would be on the owner of the purse and the . . . um . . . alleged thief." She tried to put her arm around me. "I would never have abandoned you had I known who you were."

I was still hurt and mad—Dad used to say he could see smoke coming from my ears. I started to push her arm away. But could I really blame her? After all, to Great-Granddad's Miss Drake, I'd been just another girl, maybe even a real thief. And since Miss Drake didn't recall the suspect's face, it wasn't her fault for bringing me to the kiosk. "Well, you're here now." And I leaned against her, glad she was real and solid to me again.

I was happy until a cranky Rowan popped from a row of cypress trees. "What are you idiots doing? Taking off your charms is a serious offense."

I already knew that losing my badge would get Miss Drake and me in hot water with the High Council. Miss Drake had talked about consequences and hinted that all of them would be bad.

But no one gets away with calling my dragon an idiot.

"Well, I don't see a charm on you, so you can't snitch on us, or you'll be in the same mess we are."

"But you won't be, will you, Rowan?" Miss Drake asked slowly. "I thought it was odd that a Shielder didn't accompany the group. But you're our sheepdog, aren't you?"

"Woof, woof," Rowan said. "With so many councilors on the trip, they thought an apprentice could keep an eye on things. After we got to the Exposition, I noticed you weren't in the group. It's taken me the whole day to find you."

"Shielder?" I asked.

"They enforce the High Council's decisions and watch for infractions. There are three ranks." Miss Drake's finger sketched three overlapping, inverted triangles. "The top are gold. The next are silver. And the third class are bronze."

"And the apprentices are tin." Rowan took a wallet from his pocket and opened it to show me the triangles in some dull gray metal. I guess that was tin.

My stomach did flip-flops. "Are you going to turn us in?"

"I should." Rowan put his wallet away. "But I'm not. Miss Drake saved my father from prison."

Miss Drake leaned her head to the side as she studied

him. "Was your father's name Gilbert by any chance? Gilbert the Guardian?"

"Yes," Rowan replied. His eyes shifted as if he was even more cautious now. "He told me all his other pals turned their backs on him, but you came at night and used your fire to melt the bars to his cell and then his chains."

"The iron was a very poor grade—just like his friends." Miss Drake held her hands up like a picture frame. "I thought you looked familiar. You have your brother's forehead and eyes."

It's funny, but that seemed to make him angry because he balled his hands into fists. "Is that so?"

Just then, shrill police whistles interrupted us, and I got scared. "They're coming for me."

Miss Drake glanced at her watch. "No, the Heart of Kubera should be missing by now. The police will be focused on that and not a purse snatcher."

"How did I wind up with the purse in the first place?" I wondered.

"I think when someone shouted 'purse snatcher,' the actual thief threw it away. It was your bad luck that the purse wound up by you." Miss Drake cupped her chin in her palm. "The real question is how your badge came off. When I fix a magical charm to someone, it stays fixed."

I love Miss Drake, but sometimes I wish she'd admit that she wasn't perfect. "Maybe there was something wrong with the badge's pin."

"You better tell me what happened so I know how to cover things up." Rowan didn't look at us when he spoke. Just like at the party, his eyes kept darting from side to side. I thought he was bored with us, but now I realized he had been checking for threats.

"You'd break your oath to the Council for us?" Miss Drake asked.

"My father always hoped to repay his debt to you, but he never got the chance. So now I have to do it for him."

When Miss Drake and I were done telling him our story—except for the career advice to Mrs. Wilder—he bit his lip thoughtfully.

"Do you know where your charm is, Miss Drake?"

"Yes, I hid it not far away," she said.

"Then the both of you had better go to the sand lot before you can do any more damage." He pointed toward a row of flowers. "You'll find my charm at the base of the third poppy from the left. Winnie should time-phase before anything else happens to her."

"Don't you need it?" I asked.

"I'm going to go to the kiosk to find your badge." Rowan tapped his chest where his badge had been. "All the badges look the same, so no one will know we

88

exchanged them. As long as my aunt has the same number of badges we came with, she won't care."

Relief flooded through me. "Thanks." Then a new thought came to me. "But how am I going to find your badge? And how are you going to find mine? Aren't they still invisible?"

"My aunt anticipated that problem in case someone lost their charm, so it's part of the spell," he explained. "The charm deactivates when it loses contact with a body and becomes visible. It activates again when someone puts it back on and becomes invisible. Which is why it would be so dangerous to leave yours lying around until the spell on it wears off at midnight."

"You could be stranded," Miss Drake warned.

He shrugged. "The High Council will send Shielders to get me eventually. Don't worry. I'll tell them the lost badge is mine."

"There would be 'consequences' even for a tin boy," Miss Drake said.

He stared at my dragon defiantly, his eyes as murky as Loch Ness. "It's what my father would want me to do."

Miss Drake gave him a polite nod. "Consider his debt paid in full."

I was glad Miss Drake hadn't turned him into charcoal after all. "You're actually okay," I told him.

His eyes kept watching the people passing by as if he

were trying to ignore me. "What do you mean? I'm the same as always."

I wasn't going to let him get away with that. "No, you're not. When we first met you, you were a snot."

His lips twitched up briefly into a smile as if I didn't understand how funny I was being. "It's called 'focusing on my job.'"

"Speaking of your job, is there someone you were specifically keeping an eye on?" Miss Drake asked.

Rowan was smart enough not to patronize Miss Drake like he had me. "You know I can't talk about that. I'm taking enough of a risk to help you right now. And people aren't supposed to know I'm a tin boy, so you can't tell anyone."

"You have our word," Miss Drake said, "and thank you."

After he left for the kiosk, I went to the flowerbed, but Miss Drake wouldn't let me dig until she stood in front of me, blocking the view of any passersby.

"All right," she said, "now no one will see you when you disappear."

I dug in the spot Rowan had said, and I thought what an exasperating boy he was. "Who was his father, and why did he owe you?"

"His father was a wizard who had great skill but very

poor luck. As for why he was in jail," Miss Drake said, "you'll have to ask Rowan."

"Yeah, like that'll work." I felt the round badge hidden under a thin layer of dirt. Dusting it off, I stood up and put it on.

Though she couldn't see me now, Miss Drake spoke to the empty air. "Come with me and don't get into any more mischief, no matter how tempting."

I followed her about twenty yards away, where she had stashed her charm in a bush. She slipped behind it, the branches screening her from view. When she appeared, I could see the badge pinned to her collar and knew she was synchronized with me again.

She looked me over and said, "Someone is going to notice your hat, gloves, and jacket are missing. I better fix that."

Hidden from the view of others, she swiftly moved her hands and fingers as if weaving invisible threads, and with a brief chant, she created my missing clothing for me. "Let's return to the sand lot. I've had enough time travel for one day."

"You and me both," I said.

Chapter Eight

Solving a mystery is like running a high-hurdles race.
As soon as you clear one, there's another ahead of you.

MISS DRAKE

Beaming with relief, Willamar met us just as Winnie and I crossed the line of stakes marking his future home. "You had us all so worried, dear ladies," he said, and wrapped his arms around the both of us.

As the saying goes, "Better a hug from a boa constrictor than a troll." Trolls simply do not know their own strength.

Fortunately, we dragons are born wrestlers. When we're newly hatched, our limbs are too weak to carry our weight at first. Of necessity, we slither everywhere on our bellies, and as is the custom, I spent afternoons in the clan nursery with cousins of the same age. So I learned to escape their coiling grips before I could even walk or swim.

Even in my human form, it is difficult to hold me because I'd picked up a few tricks from my stay in Mongolia, where wrestling is a national pastime. When I saw Willamar's arm curling toward me, I raised both my forearms close against my torso so the circle of his arms was larger than it needed to be. Then, by easing my own arms down to my sides and shifting my feet and hips, I could slip away. The next moment, I'd plucked Winnie from his grasp.

While I straightened her hair and clothes, I said, "We got lost, and by the time we knew where we were, it was too late to see the theft, so we headed here."

Willamar knew it was a lie, of course.

But a troll in Willamar's position would prefer my fiction to facts. Ultimately, Willamar and the other time-traveling councilors were responsible for letting Winnie and me run amok in the past. My explanation would spare them a lot of embarrassment.

Exactly as I had anticipated, Willamar sounded grateful. "How awful for you! Please, you must restore your spirits." He indicated the rear of his property, where a canvas tarp with a time badge held quite a credible spread of cheeses, crackers, cookies, and fruit along with small bottles of juice and other beverages.

Then, while he left to talk to the other councilors and make sure we all shared the same story about my misadventures, Winnie and I headed for the food.

"Miss Drake, we missed your sharp eyes at the ball." Silana dipped a strawberry into a glass of champagne.

I tried to change the subject. "Yes, I'm devastated. Did you discover who stole the Heart of Kubera?"

Silana lifted the strawberry by its stem and nibbled its side. "No, it was just like the newspapers reported. One moment, the Heart of Kubera was sparkling on Lady Gravelston while she waltzed with Senator Bradley, and the next moment—poof!—it was gone." She added, "But the greater mystery is, what happened to you?"

"We got lost," Winnie said quickly.

"Oh, my, Miss Drake, I thought you went to the Exposition almost every day." Silana swirled the strawberry around in her glass. "How could you forget where things were?" Pretending to be shocked, she raised her eyebrows, and her mouth made a little circle. "Unless . . . oh, you poor old thing. Are you going senile?"

No doubt Silana would have a delicious time telling everyone that I had become a doddering old fool.

I narrowed my eyes in warning. "Haven't you heard the proverb, 'You only tease a dragon once'? It's carved into many a fool's tombstone."

Silana smiled maliciously. "No, I hadn't, but since it's carved in stone, that's one thing you won't be able to forget." She turned away then, no doubt eager to spread her slander about me.

Winnie grabbed my sleeve so I couldn't follow the sorceress. "Don't get into a fight. We don't want any more attention."

"Don't exaggerate. I was simply going to teach her a lesson in etiquette." I tried to shake free, but Winnie wouldn't let go. "After all, what if she insults a dragon who doesn't have my vast store of patience?" I added, "And don't roll your eyes at me, young lady! One day, they'll lock while you're looking upward, and you'll never be able to see your feet again."

"Ah," Sir Isaac said as he got a plate, "but always gazing skyward is perfect for an astronomer."

Lady Louhi, though, wasn't in the mood to tease us. "Have you seen my nephew, Miss Drake? I seem to have misplaced him."

I assumed that Rowan had told her that he was going to search for us, and this was her discreet way of asking us what had happened. Her worry seemed genuine, so perhaps she really had adopted Rowan as a kind of nephew.

"Yes," I said, mentally crossing my claws. "He'll be here soon. I wouldn't worry. He struck me as someone who can take care of himself."

Rowan was not only capable but had a sense of duty as strong as Caleb's. I might have admired him except for one problem: I remembered Gilbert the Guardian only having one son, and that one was long dead—yet Rowan seemed devoted to the wizard. The evening kept piling up one mystery after another.

"Sometimes I think he tries too hard." Lady Louhi sighed.

"The boy wants to win his spurs." Sir Isaac began to heap cookies on the plate.

"So give. Did your stuff work? Did you see the thief?" Winnie asked him.

"We won't know until Lady Louhi and I analyze our recordings." He offered us the plate of cookies, but Lady Louhi simply shook her head. She had no appetite for snacks while Rowan was missing. Then he added in a low voice, "But an intriguing thought occurred to me when we returned: What if the thief didn't come from 1915? Instead, what if one of our fellow time travelers is the real thief? He or she took off their badge and cast an invisibility spell upon themselves so no one from the club would see him or her. Most likely the Council of that time only investigated magicals from 1915, not the future."

Winnie started to reach for a tart but hesitated, then reluctantly picked up an apple. Her mother, Liza, had been dropping hints that we needed to eat healthier. "Wouldn't the Fellowship see one of its members stealing the Heart of Kubera?"

Sir Isaac's eyes shone, and I wondered if he had been this excited when he had discovered gravity. "Ah, my dear Burton, not if the thief used an invisibility spell beforehand—once the badge was off, the jewel could be plucked from around Lady Gravelston's throat."

I disengaged Winnie's hand from my cuff and picked up a small plate with a slice of Black Forest cake. Liza could lecture her daughter on human nutrition all she liked, but a dragon doesn't survive thirty centuries by eating like a rabbit. "You would have noticed someone was missing—I mean, besides Rowan and us."

Sir Isaac had an odd way of eating a cookie, turning it so he could take mouse-like nibbles from around its edge. "I can account for the ones like Willamar, who remained with Lady Gravelston, but when we got to the ball, Lady Luminita said she was going to follow her prime suspect."

"Schmidt the waiter?" Winnie asked through a mouthful of apple.

Sir Isaac wagged the now thumb-size cookie at her. "That's the fellow. When the lady went off on her own, many of the others also decided to trail their choices. So you see, since we lost track of them, they could have done anything they wanted."

I got a fork. "Silana thinks the thief is a magical, so did she follow one of the ballgoers or did she follow one of the club members?"

Sir Isaac popped the cookie into his mouth. "All I can say is that Silana wasn't with us."

Perhaps there was something to Sir Isaac's theory. I wouldn't put it past her to fool everyone and take it herself.

"Well," I said, "if anyone can identify the thief, it's going to be you or Lady Louhi."

He merely grunted. "The proof of the pudding will be in the eating."

"And the cake too." I put a forkful of dessert into my mouth, and the sweetness instantly rejuvenated me so I began to feel at least twenty—no make that thirty years younger. The cake was that delicious, just like all of

Willamar's bounty. Winnie watched wistfully as I took another bite.

An anxious-looking Lady Louhi peeked at the watch pinned to her dress. "If you'll excuse me," she said, and she drifted to the street-side edge of the property to wait for her nephew. Sir Isaac kept her company.

The other time travelers ignored them, too intent on arguing about the identity of the thief and the method of the theft.

Winnie whispered to me. "I don't think the trip solved anything."

"Well, you can't expect them to give up their hobby just like that," I replied softly. But a different puzzle seemed more important to me than the stolen jewel. The pin on Winnie's badge might have been defective as she had suggested, but the pin had looked fine when I'd handled it. It bothered me that my inattention to some details had almost gotten my pet arrested and risked changing our time line.

Nearly midnight, traffic had thinned in the streets, but it hadn't completely disappeared. Willamar had begun pacing along the string boundary line while Lady Louhi and Sir Isaac stood, keeping a vigil for Rowan.

Suddenly we saw Rowan running, his long coat flapping behind him like wings. On the tan leather, I saw a bright round dot that must have been Winnie's badge because he was passing straight through pedestrians or vehicles. He had a curious bouncing gait, bounding slightly into the air with each stride as if on springs, but he covered an amazing amount of ground with each second in his race against time.

Lady Louhi waved her arm as she shouted, "Hurry, hurry!"

The other club members got to their feet and began urging Rowan on as if we were at a track meet.

He was still half a block away when I glanced at my watch.

"Is he going to make it?" Winnie asked nervously.

I shook my head.

"Help your nephew," Lorelei called to Lady Louhi. "Don't you know some kind of transportation spell?"

"Yes, but I'm forbidden to use it here," Lady Louhi said helplessly.

"Someone, anyone," Lorelei begged.

Enough was enough. I would risk the High Council's wrath. "Stand close in front of me," I whispered to Winnie.

For once, she obeyed without peppering me with a

dozen questions first. I barely moved my lips and fingers as I murmured the spell.

At Rowan's next step, he suddenly soared high into the air like a giant grasshopper, landing just within the cords and stakes.

He looked as shocked as everyone else. He stared at the street and then the sand where he was standing. "How . . . ?"

"What an amazing run!" Willamar pounded him on his back and then called to the rest of us, "Wasn't it everyone?"

The other councilors nodded. Like my being lost, Rowan's mad dash was going to become a convenient truth.

Rowan stood there panting as the world of 1915 began to quiver, and the ground grew spongy. I had the feeling of being turned inside out and wrung like an old dishrag, and then I was staring at the walls of Willamar's parlor once more.

We were back in our time again—with more mysteries to solve than ever. And very bothersome mysteries to boot!

CHAPTER NINE

I wish—*two words that can spark
an adventure or turn one topsy-turvy.*

Winnie

I sighed with relief as we entered our house. "Phew,
time travel's like any long trip. It's fun once you get
there and once you get home, but it's the traveling part
that I don't like." I grinned at Miss Drake. "But at least
we got away with it."

"It would seem so,"
Miss Drake said as
she stretched. "But
there's something
still bothering me."

"Not my badge again," I groaned as I hung up my jacket in the hallway closet. "You checked the one that Rowan found, and there was nothing wrong with it."

"And there was nothing wrong when I put it on you," Miss Drake insisted.

I'd met mules at stables, and none of them had been half as stubborn as my dragon. "Then maybe the spell only partly worked on my badge. There's bound to be one dud when Lady Louhi made so many." I added with a grin, "Or the badge was allergic to me and jumped off."

Miss Drake frowned. "You're getting sleepy, and that's making you very silly. So go to bed and we'll open the time capsule tomorrow."

Bed was sounding like a good idea after a long, exciting evening. Besides, my costume was getting itchy. But I turned to Great-Granddad Caleb's portrait, which had started our whole adventure.

The man in the business suit was older and had less hair, but I saw now that his eyes had the same kindness that I remembered in the boy's—but maybe sadder.

I rubbed at the dried water spots that I had left on the glass. "Not a chance. Now that I met him, I want to see what he wanted to leave me."

"Don't expect much," Miss Drake warned. "He was only eleven."

We went down to Miss Drake's apartment in the basement. I couldn't resist taking one of my keys from my pocket and opening her door. Great-Aunt Amelia had left me the original, and I'd made a zillion copies so I could go in anytime I liked. It still annoyed Miss Drake sometimes.

Tonight, though, she seemed grateful that she didn't have to hunt for hers. "I don't suppose you'd like a cup of tea first?" she asked. That was her way of saying she wanted one.

I was too impatient, though. The whole evening had been leading up to this. I fell to my knees by the coffee table where a rusty old square tin cookie box sat. On the lid was a picture of steamboats in the San Francisco Bay. "I'm not thirsty. Let's get this puppy open."

"Wait. Before I forget, this is also for you," she said, handing me a bundle she had made from her handkerchief.

Untying the knot, I gave a yelp. "Pink sand! How did you get it?"

"When we were in real time, I put two handfuls in my handkerchief," she told me. "I figured if the scones from now could make it there, whenever I was able to snatch some sand, I'd carry it in my pocket. It was an experiment."

"So much for always obeying the rules," I said, grasping her treasure.

"One of my rules," she reminded me, "is to always wear clothing with deep pockets." The next moment she disappeared in a golden haze, and when it cleared, she was a dragon again. "Ah, scales are so much more comfortable than human clothing."

I was eager to get inside the time capsule, but the lid seemed stuck when I pulled at it, so I drummed my fingers on the top. "Open it, open it," I said in rhythm to my tapping.

"It might be rust from the foggy air," Miss Drake said. She slipped the tip of her claw into the thin line between the can and the lid. There was a loud, screechy creak as she pried it loose.

"There it goes," she said, giving me the tin. "I'll leave the honors to you."

As I lifted the lid, I took a deep breath of the century-old air inside. Great-Granddad's air.

Despite Miss Drake's warning, I had been expecting something amazing, but on the very top was a bunch of postcards like the giant typewriter and the Tower of Jewels. Below them was an old sock. Picking it up by the toe, I shook out some brass commemorative coins and a miniature lucky horseshoe.

Miss Drake lifted an opening-day badge with a blue-yellow-and-red-striped ribbon and a closing-day badge with a picture of a woman waving good-bye. Miss Drake smiled, as if it brought back memories, and then she set them on the pile of souvenirs I'd found.

At the very bottom was a bundle of felt, an old pennant with the Tower of Jewels on it. Even though I was careful when I unrolled it, red paint flaked off, and something fell onto my lap. It was the whistle with the mongoose etched and painted on the side.

Miss Drake sighed. "So that's what happened to it."

We were learning how to play the recorder in music class, so I put it to my lips. I blew softly, and the notes of the scale floated around us. It still worked. Slowly, I played the beginning of "Molly Malone."

Miss Drake put her paws on her lap. "You play better than Caleb did. I only heard him blow the whistle at the fair and once more when we got home—but never again."

I set the whistle down on the table to keep as a souvenir of tonight. Miss Drake picked it up and examined it in her paws. "It *is* ivory," she said, "and no mere peddler crafted this. Another puzzle to ponder."

She put it on the table again.

The whistle was interesting, but I was more curious about my great-grandfather.

"If the older Caleb met me right now, what would he think?"

"That you're up way past your bedtime," Miss Drake said.

"No teasing," I begged.

She scratched her muzzle. "Hmm, he'd find you rude and rough, perhaps even a bit crude."

"Oh." My shoulders sagged, disappointed.

Miss Drake relented. "But you're no different than the other children of today, and despite all your flaws, he'd love you as much as he loved Amelia."

"Did he love Granddad Jarvis too?" I asked.

Miss Drake defended Great-Granddad. "Caleb tried to be a good father and husband, but he and his wife never saw eye to eye on his charity work." Miss Drake told me a little about some of the good things Great-Granddad had done when he had grown up. "Your great-grandmother Mary was very kind to friends and family, but she was of her class and thought the poor were stealing resources away from her children. I'm afraid that Jarvis got infected by her contempt, and that started a rift between him and his father that became a canyon over time. Sometimes things happen that way." I could see that Miss Drake regretted it, though.

Granddad Jarvis had been mean enough to chase

Mom and me all over the country so he could take me away from her. But I had to be fair. "Granddad has been trying hard to be nice in his note cards to me," I said. He'd left Mom and me alone in exchange for letters from me.

Miss Drake nodded slowly. "Caleb would like that."

Once we had put everything back in the time capsule, I took it upstairs to the second floor, where my bedroom was. I took out the whistle and then put the box in my closet before I went over to my special shelf. I put all the souvenirs from my adventures with Miss Drake on it—like a phoenix feather that glowed softly in the dark, a misty piece from the veil of Iris the rainbow goddess that floated in the air and other neat treasures. It was like my own museum of wonders.

I checked my bookcase too, and all my Little House Books were still there. So I hadn't changed the past enough to change the future. Or the Council had fixed things for me. Maybe Mrs. Wilder thought I was just a dream. But I remembered meeting her and hearing her intend to do some writing that would count. Hmmmm.

I set the whistle on the shelf and then texted Mom.

All the riders on her trip had had to turn in their phones, so she would read it with all my other texts when they got to their destination.

Met G-G Caleb 2nite. Nice guy.

What would Mom make of that? I couldn't help grin-ning as I pictured her face.

I thought the message to Mom marked the end of my adventure. But it was only the beginning.

Things seemed peaceful enough on Sunday. I had brunch with Miss Drake, finished my homework, left another message for Mom, and late that afternoon made gingerbread men with Vasilisa for the school's bake sale.

Vasilisa, our housekeeper, did all the cooking. Since her family worked in other magical homes, she knew all sorts of funny, homey gossip. I learned, for instance, that Willamar loved tutti-frutti ice cream, so tubs of it filled a special freezer.

On the windowsill, looking well fed and content, was Vasilisa's little wooden doll. Small Doll actually did all the cleaning in the house, and all she asked was that we share our meals with her—though she was crazy for chocolate and would wolf down any that came into the house.

Small Doll's world was a lot simpler than mine . . . or Laura Ingalls Wilder's. "Vasilisa," I asked, "if you wanted to do something that counts, what would that be?"

Vasilisa was humming some slow tune with a lot of deep, bass notes while she sifted flour into a bowl. She stopped as she thought for a moment. "I wish I could come up with the recipe for the perfect cake. No one could resist it, and yet it would add no calories." She sighed. "But some people are allergic to gluten. So there is no perfect cake, is there?"

"I guess not," I said, disappointed.

Vasilisa glanced into a container. "Little Madame, we need more sugar. Would you get it for me?" She nodded to a cabinet. "It's on the top shelf."

The kitchen walls were eight feet high, and the cabinet's top shelf was near the ceiling. So I dragged a chair over. Climbing it, I stretched my arm up. That was when I casually said, "I wish I had something to make me taller."

Suddenly I heard a scratching sound like claws on a floor, and from the corner of my eye, I saw a tan blur. But when I blinked, I didn't see or hear anything more. And then I was just too busy baking to wonder about it.

Later, when we had put all the cookies in cellophane bags and wrapped them tight with colored ribbon, I went up to my room.

I opened the door, and the moonlight showed a strange mound squatting in the middle of the floor. Something gleamed at me. I might have thought they were eyes, but these were square.

When I turned on the light, I saw it was a collection of junk, including a rusty old pogo stick, a broken pair of wooden stilts, a brand-new footstool, a rickety paint-splattered stepladder, and even some torn sheet music with the title "I'll Build a Stairway to Paradise."

Had someone broken into our house? But what burglar leaves his garbage behind?

Then, on the very top of the pile, I saw what had been shining at me. It was two gold buckles on a familiar pair of high-heeled shoes.

How on earth did Sir Isaac's shoes wind up on top of a pile of trash? And was he walking around barefoot at this very moment?

I hoped my teacher had some slippers handy as I put the shoes into my backpack. I'd return them to him tomorrow. Sir Isaac would like another strange puzzle to solve besides who stole the Heart of Kubera.

I didn't realize it right then, but Miss Drake and I were being pulled into a real tangled mess.

CHAPTER TEN

You don't want to know the ingredients for two things: sausages and wishes.

Winnie

Monday morning, when I went to school, I saw someone on the corner. Even if I hadn't seen his face, I would have recognized Rowan from the way he stood even straighter than the streetlamp.

Were we in trouble for losing my charm after all?

"Did the High Council send you for me and Miss Drake?" I asked him.

He shook his head as he kept scanning the area, his eyes brilliant as a clear blue pool. "Don't be stupid. After helping you cover up, I'd be in as much hot water as you."

I frowned. "Just when I thought you were okay, you had to spoil everything by calling me stupid."

He hesitated as if he were translating from one language into another. "I'm just being honest." He fell into step beside me as I crossed the street.

"Oh, yeah?" I asked skeptically. "Since you're being honest, what would you do if you wanted to do something that counted?"

"Hmm." He looked thoughtful. "Is this a quiz?"

I refused to give up. "Come on. What would you wish for?"

"To make my father proud of me." He shrugged. "Only he's gone, so that's impossible."

I wasn't having much luck with that question. So instead I asked, "Why were you waiting for me? This can't be the usual way you go to Powell, or I would have seen you before."

He dug my jacket from his backpack, dangling it in his strange, twisted fingers. "I couldn't give this to you before when the club was all around us."

So he'd found all the things I had left behind in 1915—my badge, my gloves, and the jacket with my crumpled hat tucked into one sleeve.

"Thanks." Reaching over my shoulder, I crammed everything into my backpack. "But Lady Louhi could have returned it for you."

He gave a hitch to his backpack. "Maybe I wanted to explore this part of the neighborhood."

He might be great at helping people stranded in the past, but he was a terrible fibber. Mr. Tin Boy was up to something. "Your nose is growing."

His head whipped around. "What do you mean by that?"

I shrugged as we reached the other side. "You know, the story of Pinocchio, the puppet who wanted to become a real boy but kept lying."

"I know the story says that," he said gruffly. "But why do people always accept that version? What if Pinocchio liked the way he already was?"

"Then you wouldn't have had a story." I poked a finger into his chest. "And don't try to change the subject. I just called you a liar. So tell me the truth. Why are you walking with me? Did the High Council tell you to keep tabs on me?"

I didn't like the idea of that, and I wasn't sure I

114

wanted to hang around him, even if he had helped us on Saturday.

He shoved his hands into his pockets and tried to slouch, but his stiff spine made the rest of him look like a coat hanging from a hook. "It's a free country. I can walk where I like."

"Okay," I admitted, "and since it's a free country, I don't have to talk to you."

"You're the one who started the conversation," he said defensively. His eyes flashed a gray-green like a stormy sea.

I stared at him. "I thought your eyes were—"

"They change color," he said, but offered no explanation.

For the next block, he didn't speak to me, and I didn't speak to him. And I noticed something else. Powell lay a few blocks beyond the Spriggs Academy, so there were other Powell students walking by and passing us. But both they and Rowan ignored one another. If he was as rude to them as he was to me, I couldn't blame them.

It was the opposite for me and the other Spriggs-ians. By now, they knew me enough to greet me or at least nod.

Then, about two blocks from the Academy, I saw my friend Mabli. She was in her human disguise, of course, but she was really a dwarf.

She had joined the drama club, so she had her head down while she memorized her lines from a paperback-size script. I ran and caught her shoulder in time to steer her away from a lamppost. "Careful."

She looked at me startled, like I'd just woken her up from a dream—or more like I had snatched her from the world of her play. "Oh, hi."

"How was your weekend?" I asked. I was dying to tell her about my trip through time, but that would have to wait until we were inside school, where regular humans couldn't hear us. Magicals had an agreement to hide their existence from all but a few special humans.

"Fine. I visited my grandfather down in Portola Valley and swam in his . . . pool." She leaned forward and stared at something on my other side.

When I turned, I saw Rowan had caught up with me. I didn't want Mabli jumping to the wrong conclusions. "This is Rowan. He's Lady Louhi's nephew."

"Right," Rowan said.

"Really?" Mabli asked. "I didn't know she had family in San Francisco."

"My nose isn't growing, if that's what you mean," Rowan said sharply.

Mabli drew her eyebrows together. "What?"

I leaned toward her and pretended to whisper. "Never

mind. He's got such a weird sense of humor that Lady Louhi tries to keep him secret."

Rowan shoved his hands into his pockets. "Now whose nose should be growing?"

Mabli looked at both of us, uncertain about what was going on. "Uh, ha-ha?"

When we reached the Academy's block, we met Zaina. She was also disguised as a human, but once she was inside the school, she would be able to resume her real form as a djinn.

"Hello," Mabli said, and waved a hand past me at Rowan. "This is Winnie's friend Rowan."

Almost at the same time, Rowan and I said, "We're not friends."

Mabli grinned knowingly at Zaina. "He's also Lady Louhi's nephew."

Zaina nodded. "I'm pleased to meet you." And then she winked at me.

I wanted to shout that they were both wrong if they thought there was anything between us. But Miss Drake and I had promised to keep secret Rowan's job as a Shielder, so I couldn't tell them why he was with me.

As soon as we reached the gates, though, I did a quick right turn and stormed through them without looking back.

Rowan just had to make more problems for me. "Good-bye!" he called loudly. "And thanks for Saturday. I had a lot of fun."

Even Mortimer the gargoyle, the guardian on the iron gate, twisted his head to stare at me.

Mabli hurried up beside me. "Okay, so spill."

Zaina came up on my other side. "Yeah."

"You don't know the half of it," I said. I'd originally intended to tell them about my trip, but I kept my mouth shut now. What they really wanted to hear about was Rowan—a lot of which had to stay top secret.

From their whispers and grins, my not talking only made my friends jump to the wrong conclusions.

And it must have been Be-a-Frog Day because they weren't the only ones whose minds hopped in the wrong direction.

Sir Isaac was in charge of the school bake sale, so when I got to science class, I added my cookies to the other contributions in the classroom cabinet. Then I went over to the blackboard where he was writing a formula. He didn't need chalk, though. He just drew the letters with a finger.

I'd been expecting him to wear another pair of shoes, but instead, his stocking feet were in plastic flip-flops. I guess a genius wore what he liked.

Setting my bag down, I rummaged through it to find his shoes. "Excuse me, Sir Isaac."

"Ah, Burton, have you come to warn me that you've left my realms of light to go over to the dark side with Einstein?" He finished writing the Greek letter delta and turned. "No, it seems you've come to present me with footwear instead. My own, to be precise." And he took the shoes from me. "My thanks. I was wondering what had happened to them."

"I don't know how they got there, but they were on top of a pile of junk in my room," I said.

He kicked his flip-flops into a corner. "And next you'll be telling me that your canine ate your homework."

I blinked. "Pardon?"

He frowned. "Five demerits for such a clumsy tale. A prankster's wit must match the cleverness of her jape." When he saw my blank look, he explained. "The jest you played on me."

Oh, no! He thought I had played a trick on him. My stomach tightened. In the last three centuries, Sir Isaac had turned his brainpower to practical jokes as well as science. If kings weren't safe from his stunts, what hope did I have? "But that's the truth."

Setting a hand on the desk for support, he put on his shoes and instantly grew a couple of inches taller.

"However, the score will be settled if you tell me how you removed my shoes from my closet. Did Miss Drake help you?"

I didn't think it was good to get her involved in a prank war with Sir Isaac. With her dragon pride, she might misinterpret a simple trick as an insult and retaliate with fire and fangs.

I shook my head quickly. "No, she had nothing to do with it." When I saw the gleam in his eye, I realized that he had mistaken that as a confession from me. "And neither did I," I added hastily.

But it was too little too late.

Sir Isaac saluted me with an imaginary sword. "Then a duel it shall be."

That was the last thing I wanted. "No, wait." I waved an invisible white flag. "You won."

He clicked his tongue. "When a duelist takes the first shot, she must allow her opponent to fire his pistol in return. So you must allow me to play at least one trick on you. And I will take great pleasure in deciding when and where."

I spent the rest of his class feeling like a condemned prisoner. I knew the wheels in his great mind were grinding out a plan for revenge because every now and then he would glance my way and smile slyly.

That made me desperate enough to ask Lady Louhi for help, and I rushed to her class.

She smiled at me. "You're one of the two people I wanted to see. Nessie just sent a message that she's used up all the bubble bath that you and Liri made and would like more."

On a field trip to Loch Ness, we'd brought gifts for Nessie. I was glad that she liked ours, but that wasn't my main concern right now.

"I'll talk to Liri about making more," I said, "but Sir Isaac's mad at me."

"Oh, dear," Lady Louhi said.

I didn't like the sound of that. "He thinks I played a trick on him by taking his favorite pair of shoes. You know, the ones with the gold buckles?"

"Oh, dear, dear, dear." She sounded even more concerned.

I licked my lips. "They just appeared in my room Sunday night. I don't know how. Honest. But Sir Isaac's sure that me and Miss Drake pranked him. Can you talk to him?"

"Of course." She patted my shoulder sympathetically. "But when it comes to feuds, well, Sir Isaac's like a rocket. Once you light his fuse, there's no stopping him."

I sighed. "At least, he won't try anything until he makes his report to the club."

She shook her head. "I'm afraid he's capable of juggling several projects at once."

I would have to get into a war with a genius. "I wish I had something to protect myself," I said with a groan, and thought I saw the same tan blur I had seen on Sunday in the kitchen, but it was gone in an instant. "Well," I asked, trying to drop a hint to my teacher, "do you think I can buy a charm somewhere?"

Lady Louhi spread her hands. "Without knowing the what, when, where, and how, you would need a wheelbarrow full of them, and even then they might not be enough."

I was doomed!

I turned to walk to my desk but stopped and dropped my voice low. "Well, could you help me with your nephew?"

"Did Rowan do or say something rude to you?" she asked.

"Not exactly," I admitted. "He . . . uh . . . was waiting for me and then walked with me to Spriggs."

"Oh, dear," she said again, but this time, the corners of her mouth turned up.

"I'm grateful for what he did last Saturday." The

words rushed out of me. "But this is embarrassing." I jerked my head toward my classmates. "My friends are getting the wrong idea."

"Did you tell him how you felt?" she asked.

"Yeah, but he said he was just going to Powell," I said.

"I'll have a talk with him about making you uncomfortable." Lady Louhi gave me a big smile. "But in my opinion, he hasn't done anything horrible, and he can be quite headstrong."

I thought that at least lunch would cheer me up, but when I went to see what treats Vasilisa had packed for me, I saw my locker door was bulging. Had Sir Isaac struck already?

"Watch out," I warned everyone near me.

"What's wrong?" asked Liri, my naiad friend.

"Sir Isaac said he was going to get me," I said. Instantly, the area cleared.

Then, standing as far to the side as I could, I leaned and started entering my combination to the lock. As the tumblers clicked, I thought I heard the metal door groaning as if it were under a lot of pressure. Had he put in a self-inflating rubber raft? Was it a dozen bowling balls?

The possibilities whirled through my mind, each

crazier than the last. When I'd entered the last number, I took a deep breath and gripped the handle.

By now, my friends and classmates had gathered at a careful distance.

Sometimes, all you can do is jump from the airplane, Mom had told me.

I lifted the handle. Instantly, the door swung toward me, and a football helmet with the Powell mascot, a maroon octopus, bounced across the hallway floor. A small round wooden shield with an iron rim clattered after it, along with a baseball bat, a twirling umbrella hat, and then a can of extra-strength mosquito repellent.

"Getting ready for PE?" snickered Nanette, my sorceress frenemy. Her pal Lupe, a werewolf, laughed loudly, along with several others.

Liri picked up the can quickly. "I'll help you put your stuff inside."

I waved a hand at the junk. "But this isn't mine."

"Well, how did it get into your locker?" Mabli asked, and the next moment turned to Nanette.

She stopped giggling immediately. "Hey, don't blame me. I'm still on thin ice with Ms. Griffin."

Ms. Griffin was our principal, and Nanette had gotten into trouble with her after trying to hurt me at the Halloween Festival.

"Who else would have jammed this stuff into Winnie's

locker?" Saskia demanded. She was a centaur who was always ready for a fight.

"Sir Isaac," I said. "He's getting even because he thinks I played a trick on him."

"Oog," Mabli said.

I told the others about finding his shoes and then realized something that put me in a great mood. "But now he's pranked me, and we're even."

"You really think a pile of junk and a lost lunch are enough revenge?" Liri asked.

I glanced inside my locker. The red nylon bag with the stars had been smashed flat. Whatever treats Vasilisa had packed for me were now paste.

I thought of the wonderful smells coming from the kitchen this morning. "I wish I had something to eat."

This time, I thought I heard a small whooshing sound like a small jet dashing by.

"Don't worry. I'll share with you," Mabli said.

Liri and I dumped the joke stuff into a trashcan, and Mabli opened her locker. "Hey, my lunch is gone."

"So's mine," Nanette said angrily.

Lunches were missing from five other lockers.

Liri scratched her cheek, and ripples spread across her transparent skin. "Is this another one of Sir Isaac's pranks?"

"But I didn't do anything to him," Nanette complained.

"He wouldn't pick on you for no reason. It's got to be somebody else." With a sinking feeling, I realized that maybe the junk in my locker hadn't been his work either—which meant our duel was still going on.

Nanette set her fists on her hips. "Who else did you make mad?"

"Nobody," I said, but then I thought about Rowan. He was just strange enough even if I didn't know how he might have done it.

Nanette jabbed a finger. "Ha, I can see it in your face. There is somebody."

"No," I insisted. "Come on. We can buy cafeteria lunches."

The auditorium in the basement also served as a cafeteria, and the lunch counter had pretty good food. But when we got there, we found a large group just standing around to the side of the tables.

"There's a name on this bag," Sir Isaac said from the center of the group. He must be the lunchtime proctor today. "Mabli?" His hand held a paper bag above the heads. "Where are you, Mabli?"

"How did my lunch get here?" Mabli asked.

The group parted, and I followed Mabli to the center where Sir Isaac stood. He motioned to the pile of bags and boxes.

Nanette snatched up a bento box. "That's mine."

"Someone has strange appetites." Sir Isaac nudged the bale of hay with a buckled shoe. Resting on top of the bale was a can of chicken soup, a piggy bank, and a parking meter with a stack of quarters.

I appealed to Sir Isaac. "This is what happened in my room last night. A pile of junk just appeared. And when I opened my locker just now, I had more trash inside. And now this." I motioned to the can of soup and lunches. "We can eat those, but the hay and parking meter are just more weird garbage."

Sir Isaac rested his hand against his chin. "It's refuse only if it has no purpose. Do these items have anything in common?" He spun around with a quick, abrupt motion like rubber bands snapping. "A horse would eat hay." He picked up a quarter and put it into the parking meter, which whirred and showed six minutes of time. "And a coin feeds the parking meter or a piggy bank." He pirouetted like a mad top. His eyes were shining as he dared me. "And so what do we conclude, Burton?"

"They're all things to feed someone or something." I scratched my head. "You know, before I came down here, I wished I had something to eat." Silently, I ran through the items that had been in my locker. "And all the junk—"

"Ah, careful." Sir Isaac wagged his finger at me. "Remember, it is only garbage if there is no rhyme or reason to it."

I corrected myself. "I was so worried about your revenge that I wished for something to protect me. And suddenly my locker was filled with stuff I could use for that."

"And what about last night?" Sir Isaac prompted. "Did anything else have something in common with my shoes?"

I thought aloud. "Pogo stick. Ladder." Even the music had been about stairs. "I was having trouble reaching the top of a cabinet yesterday. So I wished for something that would make me taller—like your shoes would do."

There were giggles and smiles around us that everyone instantly tried to hide from Sir Isaac. Everyone understood what the shoes did for him, but no one wanted to get on his bad side.

"Sorry," I said quickly.

"You should be," Sir Isaac said. "Why can't fashion elevate the body as well as the soul?"

I had something more to worry about besides his upcoming prank. "Someone must be granting my wishes."

"But who?" Zaina asked. As a djinn, she knew something about fulfilling wishes, though none of her family had that kind of power.

"I wish—" I caught myself before I said that I wished I knew. That might result in a pile of books and computers and—well, your guess was as good as mine.

Instead, I just shook my head. "That's the billion-dollar question."

CHAPTER ELEVEN

A well-made wish consists of 10 percent knowing what you want and 90 percent knowing how to wish for it.

⟶ MISS DRAKE ⟵

Knowing that our friends, the creatures in the neighborhood, kept an eye on Winnie, I'd stopped escorting her to and from school. But last evening, when she had shown me the debris in her room, I felt as if someone had drawn an icicle down my spine.

Perhaps it was no accident that Winnie had lost her badge after all. Some

villain might be targeting her. So I resumed sneaking from the house and flying above her in miniature form as she walked to school.

When I saw Rowan, I assumed he had come to the same conclusion based on what had happened at the Exposition and was guarding Winnie—perhaps at Lady Louhi's behest. (I was still wondering if she was truly his aunt or if it had just been a convenient ruse for him to accompany her on the trip.)

When I returned home, I thought I would have to help Small Doll carry the heavier items to the garbage cans, but she already had Winnie's floor cleared and the rug smelled faintly of soap and antiseptic spray.

So instead, I put on my human disguise and broke my fast on the upstairs patio outside of Liza's bedroom. There, with one of Vasilisa's delicious tarts in my belly and the scent of Dragon Well tea refreshing my brain, I could consider the strange events of the past few days.

Spread below me were the drab modern buildings that had replaced the delicate Persian carpet of the Exposition. A long strip of lawn, now called the Marina Green, had replaced the North Gardens, where Winnie and I had watched the fireless fireworks paint the night sky with light.

When you have lived as long as I have, you become resigned to the fact that nothing stays the same. And yet, though people and places change, general patterns persist through time, whether it is in cities, families, or events. And there is one design above all others that I can recognize: the web of treachery and deceit.

I worked out the distances in my mind, and it was possible for one of the club members to slip away from the hall, stage the purse snatching, and then return to the others. As Sir Isaac had said, the travelers had lost track of one another.

So perhaps Sir Isaac was half right. What if one of the club members had taken off his or her badge and used magic to become invisible—not to steal the jewel, but to remove Winnie's charm and drop it on the ground and then strand her back in the past by blaming her for purse stealing. Some heartless, ruthless villain was striking at me by targeting my pet.

The delicate teacup broke in my hand. I scolded myself for losing my temper. Now was a time when I needed to be as cold and calculating as our enemy.

Think!

It was bad: He or she could strike at us at will. The pile of garbage had been more than a prank. It had been a message that our adversary could enter and leave our house despite my state-of-the-art human sensors and magic wards.

But how had our opponent known where to find us at the fair?

Faced with these riddles, I turned to the most devious mind I knew, Reynard. I told him about our trip to the Exposition, omitting the fact that we had seen him as a fashion accessory. When he heard that someone had tried to harm Winnie, he immediately volunteered his services.

Will drop everything 2 find threat.

He automatically assumed one suspect:

Who else was there besides Silana?

Ever since I had saved her niece from disgrace at the Academy's Halloween festival, Silana had limited herself to verbal barbs and the occasional slander about me. It was possible, though, that she had decided to escalate our feud again.

Otherwise, as far as I knew, none of the other club members held a grudge against me, and I wrote that to Reynard. The wily fox texted:

Sum1 could b acting as agent 4 real enemy. Need
list of every1 there.

It's true that over the centuries I have stepped on a
few paws, feet, and tentacles, so it was possible that a
cowardly foe had hired a club member to do the dirty
work.

Closing my eyes, I tried to picture the near catastro-
phe at the fair in detail until that moment when a fairgoer
had spotted the purse near Winnie and shouted, "Purse
snatcher!"

Wait. She had said something before that. What
was it?

First, she had yelled "T'ief." Just as someone else with
an accent had pronounced "thief."

Check Lady Luminita.

I thanked Reynard for his help because I knew he
would make Winnie's safety a top priority. Next, after
obtaining the list of guests and servants from Willamar, I
forwarded it to Reynard and asked him to look for someone powerful and with a cruel streak.

Then I went about the house renewing my wards
and magical traps and adding more. By then, it was late

afternoon, and it was time to follow Winnie from school. But before I was about to leave, Reynard texted me:

Lady Luminita likes roulette. The roulette wheel does not like her. She owes big bucks in Monte Carlo.

It was possible our hidden foe had hired the lady to carry out his revenge. But which of my many enemies was staying in the shadows like a coward?

I left to escort Winnie, and I began to review the list of my enemies continent by continent and had worked my way through part of Africa when I reached the Spriggs Academy. There I saw Rowan, his eyes now a grayish blue to match his school blazer, standing as erect as a sentry near the entrance and ignoring the curious stares from Mortimer the gargoyle on the gate.

When the bell rang inside, Winnie's schoolmates rushed out, and in a few minutes, so did she. Saskia, Zaina, and Liri were with her, but the minute Zaina saw Rowan, she whispered to the others.

Winnie gave him a look so chilly that it should have frozen the boy into a block of ice. "Your aunt wants to see you."

"She already texted me," Rowan said. "I'll try not to

make you uncomfortable from now on." I could see he wasn't helping the situation, just antagonizing her more in front of her chums.

"Winnie," Saskia said, "aren't you going to introduce us to your friend?"

"This is Rowan, Lady Louhi's nephew." Winnie waved a hand at him curtly. "But he's not a friend. He's . . . um . . . a fellow pedestrian."

Liri waggled her fingers in a shooing motion. "Well, don't let us get in your way."

"I thought we were going to do homework together at my house?" an exasperated Winnie asked. "Vasilisa could make us snacks."

"Tempting, but we each just changed our minds." Zaina grinned.

"Amazing coincidence, isn't it?" Liri said.

"And convenient for you," Saskia added.

"Whatever you're thinking, stop it," Winnie declared. "Just stop it."

But the three of them simply waved good-bye.

Rowan cleared his throat. "I wouldn't mind something to eat."

"There's a diner five blocks away," Winnie spoke curtly. Obviously she was not in a mood to play host.

While I flew high and unnoticed above them, I

wondered if Rowan was truly infatuated with Winnie or if he was being conscientious about staying with her to protect her.

Winnie stomped along, and Rowan asked, "When I was trying to reach Willamar's lot, it was Miss Drake who helped me with a spell, wasn't it?" Winnie's silence was enough confirmation, and Rowan sighed. "Just when I thought I'd settled the debt, she's started a new one."

Winnie, though, ignored all his other attempts to start a conversation, unwilling even to exchange an opinion about the weather. I could see my pet was in uncharted waters with confusing emotions. The clever girl liked to control things, and Rowan was neither in her plans nor quite controllable.

He stopped obediently at the driveway, a forlorn figure as Winnie trudged on.

Our gardener, Paradise, was doing something botanical to a rosebush. She was a dryad whose skin was the dark, ruddy hue of her redwood trees. "Afternoon, Miss Winnie." She looked down the driveway toward Rowan. "Sir."

"Don't pay him any attention," Winnie ordered.

Then she gritted her teeth when Rowan called up to her. "Winnie, I'll see you tomorrow."

Spinning around, she shook her head at him. "I wish I had something to make you go away. Oh, no." She clapped her hands over her mouth in horror.

I thought I saw something tan streak across our property.

The next moment, a pile of trash appeared on the driveway. When Paradise picked up a handful of brochures, she said, "This first one is a set of plans for how to build a hang glider." Her large hands fanned the other brochures like cards. "And these are schedules for trains, planes, buses, and ships."

"Not again," a frustrated Winnie said.

Beneath the brochures was a pair of rusty roller blades, a red stick labeled CATTLE PROD, a jet pack, a baby carriage, and finally a very bewildered bald human wearing a dark green uniform and cap.

"Hey, Bill." Paradise helped him to his feet and then explained to Winnie, "Bill works as a chauffeur for an elf family four blocks away."

"Hi, Paradise." Bill nodded politely to Winnie. "Miss." He scratched his head as he looked around. "What did you do with my limo?"

"Nothing," Paradise said. "You're at the Burtons'."

Bill glanced at the street signs on the corner. "Well, so I am. If you'll excuse me, I'd better get home."

"What happened?" Rowan demanded.

Bill shrugged as he started down the sidewalk. "Beats me. My boss had just called to be picked up. One moment, I'm getting in the limo, and the next, I'm standing here."

"Do you remember anything else?" Rowan asked.

"Nope." Bill added, "I've had some funny things happen to me since I got this job, but nothing like this whooshing through the air." He rubbed his stomach. "It's hard on the tum-tum."

There was a sudden breeze followed by a loud crash. Now a large black car was parked on the driveway. I thought I saw the tan blur again.

Bill fished his keys from his pocket. "And there's the car. Now that's service." Touching his fingers to his cap, he said, "Excuse me, Miss Burton." Then, getting into the limousine, he waved a cheerful good-bye to Paradise and backed down the driveway.

Paradise scratched her head and toed the jet pack. "What should we do with all of this, Miss Winnie?"

Winnie started for the house. "Throw away the schedules, but put the other stuff into the shed until I can figure a way to return it all."

"You said 'not again'?" Rowan pointed at the trash. "You mean this happened before?"

"Are you asking as Lady Louhi's nephew," Winnie

139

asked over her shoulder, "or as . . . ?" The word *Shielder* floated invisibly between them.

"Or as," Rowan confirmed. When Winnie remained silent, he added, "Better talk before you have no choice."

I could have told the young fool that Winnie did not respond well to threats. True to form, she turned away from him once more. "I'll think about it."

"But it's for your own good," Rowan warned.

Jingling her keys, Winnie said, "Paradise, keep the cattle prod handy."

I hurried to reach the secret entrance in the park, seething over how our opponent was toying with us. Winnie had wished for something to make Rowan go away, and the villain had sent an eccentric collection of ways to do that.

But this was even worse news. Our nemesis could hear us wherever we were.

So, when Winnie and I met in my apartment, she told me what had happened at school and Sir Isaac's conclusions. Apparently the gargoyle guardians hadn't been able to stop our adversary any more than the school's wards, which were even stronger than mine.

Picking up my tablet, I tapped a claw on the reinforced glass and then held it up for her to read:

We'll have to return the stolen items to the owners somehow and compensate them for the inconvenience. But we have bigger problem.

When I finished writing my suspicions, Winnie took the tablet and typed:

Creepy! So someone listens 2 everything we say?

I wrote back:

I'll ask Small Doll 2 check nooks & crannies 4 electronic bugs. I'll hunt 4 magical ones.

Winnie used my tablet to promise me:

In meantime, will b careful what I wish.

I tapped:

Good rule even when enemy isn't eavesdropping.

* * *

I ran through what I had just seen on the driveway, seeking some detail that would help us. That was when I recalled that curious blur. It had also preceded the purse snatching at the Exposition. Could our opponent be using some imp to achieve his or her revenge? Our foe might have hidden it in their costume when we traveled through time and then released it to follow us.

I asked her on my tablet:

Did you see anything be4 yr wishes granted at school?

Taking the tablet, she wrote:

Only saw tan streak. 2 fast. Not sure what it was.

Neither did I, but its speed had to be the way the creature got through protective charms and wards. In the microseconds before the charm or ward could finish working, the imp was already past it. It would be like slipping through an open doorway before the door could shut and the lock could click into place to foil a burglar's entrance. But how would we catch a being that darted about like lightning?

At that velocity, the imp would barely have time to

sense the magical objects ahead of it. So it might ignore a non-magical trap, especially if that trap was so simple that it didn't even look like one. Perhaps I could transform the creature's greatest strength—its speed—into its greatest weakness.

Suddenly I recalled a trick that a Chinese taro farmer in Hawaii had used to deal with pests.

With my tablet, I explained what I wanted Winnie to do and then showed the message to her.

When she nodded in understanding, I went into the kitchen and began to work on something that would stick to more than the creature's ribs.

CHAPTER TWELVE

Wishes are like eating peanuts.
It's hard to stop with just one.

⟶ Winnie ⟵

I rolled up Miss Drake's old rug and put it in her bedroom. I couldn't wait to catch the imp that had been making so much trouble for me.

Then Miss Drake carried a big pot of thick goo from the kitchen and set it down on the bare floorboards.

She used her tablet to warn me:

Do NOT get
superpaste on u.

I sniffed it cautiously and then borrowed her tablet to write:

What's in it?

Rice with other sticky ingredients. In old days, Chinese used rice paste 4 kites. This is improved version. Farmer in Hawaii caught big cockroaches with it. Some 3 inches long.

I didn't want to imagine what one looked like. "Ugh," I automatically said aloud. And she quickly agreed, tapping:

Ugh, indeed. But they didn't move once they stepped on paper. Neither will our pest.

We used spoons to drop the goop onto sheets of paper and smear it around until the whole surface was sticky.

I knew the stuff worked real good after I got some on my fingers. I couldn't pull them apart until Miss Drake wrote that I should spit on them. The paste dissolved enough for me to spread my fingers again.

After that, I was more careful putting the paste on the paper while Miss Drake shrank to about a yard in length and flew around her living room and placed the paper on the floor. We did that again and again until the floor was covered with sheets of the wet, sticky paper. The sofa became our little island, where we huddled in a white sticky sea.

Miss Drake's claws tapped on her tablet:

Wish 4 something.

When you can have anything in the world, what do you ask for? I could have had my personal pair of koala bears or panda cubs or the latest video games—and assorted junk to go with it. Of course, later, everyone and everything would have to be returned.

At that moment, my stomach growled a hint to me. "I wish for a lot of snacks," I said, wondering if a vending machine would match Miss Drake's color scheme.

Then I held my breath and crossed my fingers. Since I'd gotten my dragon, I did a lot of that. Even grocery shopping was exciting because Miss Drake liked to get her stuff from a shop up in the clouds. I bet she had never even gone into a supermarket.

Miss Drake's eyes narrowed, her whole body tensed, and the tip of her tail twitched back and forth, but she would have been annoyed if I told her she looked like a cat getting ready to pounce.

Suddenly the paper sheets by the door whipped into the air and began to spin around until they became a white whirlwind. The next moment, the sofa shook as Miss Drake sprang from it, her wings flaring outward as she swooped toward the commotion. Then she hovered as her hind paws held up a wriggling ball of paper.

"Got you!" she cried.

"Let Nanu Nakula go!" a muffled voice said.

Though the trapped creature was a lot smaller than Miss Drake, my dragon had trouble holding on to it. It seemed like the paper tangle was swinging her around so that her wings knocked over a jar full of fancy pens and bottles of ink.

When she tipped over the antique clock on the mantle, though, she lost her temper. "Hold still or I'll use you for a punching bag."

The bundle grew quiet. "Nanu Nakula cannot move in here. Is that a fair fight?"

"Of course not, because life itself isn't fair." Miss Drake pulled off a sheet of paper. "Now don't move until we get a good look at you," she warned, and began peeling the paper away like the layers of an onion. The last piece came away with some tan fur.

"Ow! Ow! Ow! You scalped Nanu Nakula, nāgī!"

Dangling from Miss Drake's claws, the wish-granting creature was about the size of a mouse but very thin with a long furry tail. His soft fur was a pale brown flecked with spots of gold, but his chest fur was a reddish color like an English robin. His forepaws clutched a celery stick—a snack for me, I guessed.

I leaned forward to stare. "Hey, he looks sort of like the carving on the side of Great-Grandpa's whistle."

"Release Nanu Nakula!" the very tiny mongoose said to Miss Drake and jabbed the celery at me. "Look at her. She's skin and bones. Nanu Nakula must feed her."

"That overgrown piece of grass won't fill her up." Miss Drake sniffed. She did love her cookies and cakes.

"Nanu Nakula was just starting the harvest." The mongoose waved the celery like a sword. "Anyway, it wouldn't do you any harm to eat healthy, you nāgī nag."

It's always important to stick up for your friends. "Miss Drake's a dragon," I corrected him. "She's not one of those whatchamacallits."

"I've fought enough nāgas to know one when I see one." The mongoose used the celery as a pointer. "Body thin like a giant cobra and a face like an old boot—only a nāgī could be this ugly."

"Nāgas don't have wings, but I do," Miss Drake said, and flapped them noisily.

The mongoose craned his head to the side and saw her wings reflected in a mirror. "Nanu Nakula will give you this much: you have a very clever disguise, nāgī."

When Miss Drake lowered her head, I thought she was going to pop him into her mouth like a snack, but she stopped an inch away from the mongoose. "We don't have time for games. Who sent you to spy on Winnie?" She made a point of showing her fangs.

The mongoose wasn't scared at all by the difference in their sizes. Instead, he thumped the celery against her muzzle. "As if Nanu Nakula would tell his enemy anything."

Then I knew what I should have asked for in the first place. "Cancel the snacks. I wish for a card or something with your master's name on it." That would give us all the proof we needed.

The mongoose jerked a free paw at Miss Drake. "The nāgī will have to let go of Nanu Nakula first."

"And have to trap you all over again?" Miss Drake laughed harshly. "Not likely."

The mongoose spoke slowly for emphasis. "Get . . . out . . . of . . . Nanu Nakula's . . . way."

"And who will make me? You?" Miss Drake dared him.

"Yes—Nanu Nakula!" With a sudden thrust, the mongoose shoved the celery between Miss Drake's lips, and it dangled like a green cigar.

Miss Drake reared in surprise, and he broke free from her claws, throwing himself hind paws first at her scales. Bouncing off her, he soared through the air and dived into my backpack.

"Hey," I said as he squirmed under the flap.

The next moment, he reappeared with my student ID. Hopping onto my lap, he held it up to me. "The nāgī has bewitched you and stolen your memories, poor master. Such a cheat. Such a liar. Even Heaven despairs of reforming her."

I took the card. "I'm not your master."

The mongoose gave a little bow. "Yes, you are. You are Nanu Nakula's one and only master. He has waited a hundred years in the attic to be summoned." The mongoose made it sound like it was my fault.

Miss Drake spat out the celery as she circled overhead, ready to pounce. "Small Doll must not bother cleaning up there, but someone would have heard you going bump in the night."

The mongoose jumped onto my palm. He was just the right size to fit in the hollow. "Because Nanu Nakula was Beautiful and Beautiful is never Helpful, and Helpful is never Beautiful." The mongoose's hind paws began to tickle my palm as he twirled around. "Then you blew the whistle, and he became Helpful once more. Beautiful is silent and still, but Helpful must be quick, quick, quick."

"He must change from something else to a mongoose

each time someone plays the whistle," Miss Drake said thoughtfully.

So the whistle's like a remote control. I was curious. "I wish for my great-granddad's whistle." I added quickly, "And just the whistle."

Instantly, he became a tan blur, leaping from my palm, and soared above the sticky paper on the floor. He used Miss Drake as a trampoline to jump over to the door and then under it.

Before my dragon could complain, he was on my palm, holding up the whistle in both paws. "Oh, the loveliness of Nanu Nakula! He dazzles. He enthralls. Mightiest of all mongooses. Kings and queens fight wars for him. But Nanu Nakula belongs to you and only to you. So rejoice. Play the whistle!"

Lifting the whistle to my lips, I blew several notes on it, and with each note, he began to pirouette faster and faster until he was a blur again. Suddenly there was a flash of red light, and on my lap was a large pendant of a golden mongoose with a ruby the size of a quail's egg.

"The Heart of Kubera," Miss Drake gasped.

The ruby in the gold mongoose's chest flickered with light from without and within. It was a rich bright red, radiant and pulsing like a beating heart, almost with a life of its own.

I pointed the whistle at the pendant. "So this is when he's Beautiful. And when he's a mongoose, he must be Helpful."

Miss Drake rubbed her muzzle as she studied it. "At the Exposition, Nanu Nakula was a pendant around Lady Gravelston's neck, but when Caleb blew on the whistle that first time, he changed into the mongoose once again, left the ball, and tracked Caleb, even though we were invisible."

I snapped my fingers. "No one stole the Heart of Kubera because he stole himself. But then why didn't Caleb get into a mess with wishes like I did?"

"He made the time capsule the next day. I guess he just didn't happen to make any wishes before then." Miss Drake shrugged. "I assume the mongoose had hidden in the attic to wait. But Caleb must have blown the whistle one more time before he put it in the box, but that was enough to change the mongoose into the pendant for another hundred years—hidden so well not even Small Doll could find it."

I started to grow excited. "You mean if I had wished for a fortune, the mongoose would have brought me gold and jewels instead of stuff to make me taller?"

"Yes," Miss Drake warned, "but the mongoose doesn't make them from thin air. He steals them." She tapped a claw against her muzzle. "Nāgas and mongooses are mortal enemies. I suspect a wizard or sorceress copied Kubera's mongoose and created this pest to raid nāga treasure vaults just as a normal mongoose would raid a chicken coop."

"But why give him two forms?" I asked.

Miss Drake spread her paws. "Perhaps it was to avoid trouble like you got into with casual wishes. And if the mongoose has to have another shape, why not make it something pretty to see? Somehow long ago the whistle got separated from the pendant, and then people forgot that the whistle controlled the Heart of Kubera. Over time, everyone just thought of the pendant as simply a beautiful piece of jewelry."

"So it was just an accident that the whistle wound up at the fair?" I asked.

"More like serendipity . . . fate reuniting it with the Heart of Kubera," Miss Drake said, and continued. "A sailor brought it there on purpose. I think he knew it was magical but had no clue about its power or real secret. If he had, he wouldn't have sold it to the stall keeper."

I remembered how frantic the stall keeper had been. "But Great-Granddad bought it before the stall keeper could use it."

Miss Drake nodded. "The stall keeper must have died a bitter, frustrated man."

I stared down at the pendant. "So what do we do with

the Heart of Kubera? Return him to Lady Gravelston's family?"

She tapped a claw on her muzzle. "Well, her ancestor stole him from the Manchus in China, but the Manchus had stolen it from someone else, so who knows to whom it truly belongs? I suppose we'll have to hold on to him until I decide the proper thing to do."

"In the meantime, shouldn't we tell the club?" I asked, picturing Sir Isaac's face when we solved the theft. Maybe he'd even forget our duel and let me be.

Miss Drake must have imagined Sir Isaac's reaction too because she smiled. "Yes, I'll ask Willamar to call a meeting." She reached for the pendant. "Until then, I'll lock up Mr. Beautiful where he can't do any harm."

I thought of the poor mongoose trapped as a pendant all those centuries before the Exposition and then another hundred years afterward. That didn't seem right.

And maybe I could do something good for everybody. Something that counted!

So before Miss Drake could stop me, I set the whistle to my lips and blew.

✎∽ MISS DRAKE ✎∽

I have always liked a little spirit in my pets, but unfortunately, Winnie had spirit by the barrelful. The pendant twirled like a top until it was a red streak. "Leave it alone," I ordered. "No more wishes!"

"But this isn't just for me. It's for everybody," Winnie promised. The spinning red blur turned brown . . . tan, until the mongoose was standing on her palm, bouncing up and down eagerly on his hind paws.

"Nanu Nakula lives to be Helpful. Please tell him what you want, master," he begged.

"I wish for world peace," Winnie said.

I was touched by such a generous wish—one worthy of Caleb. Right now the impulse was just a seed but worth nurturing and encouraging to grow.

Instead of darting off, though, the mongoose's forepaws ruffled the fur on his head in frustration. "Gold Nanu Nakula can grab. Diamonds he can hold. But peace he cannot carry."

Winnie's finger stroked the mongoose's head, trying to calm him down. "Okay, okay, I take back my wish."

"Now change him into Mr. Beautiful," I ordered urgently.

The mongoose started to tremble. "No, no. Nanu Nakula is Helpful."

Winnie didn't raise her whistle. "Poor little guy, he's shaking." Her finger stroked his side. "You don't like being cooped up as a pendant, do you?"

The mongoose shook his head violently. "No, no. Nanu Nakula lives, but he cannot move. He cannot see. He can only hear. Year after year."

Winnie shuddered. "It's like being buried alive."

He'd had a lot of masters over the centuries, and probably every one of them had kept him in his Beautiful form so he couldn't create mischief.

I was beginning to understand what made the mongoose tick, so I spoke to him in Sanskrit. "Dost thou understand me, Nanu Nakula?"

The mongoose's head jerked around. "So thou speakest the language of the gods, O sly nāgī."

I had been careful to use the accent of the highest caste, the priests. "I warn thee for the last time: I am no nāgī. Dragon am I, and know I what the stars sing to burn away the dark and the cold. One word of star song and thy ears would shrivel, and thy toes curl."

The mongoose gazed up at me unafraid. "Dragon thou may or may not be, but thou art surely a creature of power and knowledge. And so Nanu Nakula shall make a small peace with thee. He will not call thee nāgī."

I hovered over him. "Nor art thou as simple as thou pretendest to be."

"How so?" He folded his paws, the picture of innocence.

The bantam confidence artist didn't fool me one bit, though. "Thou knew Lady Winnie desired a ladder, yet thou found the imperfections in her wish and gave her pogo sticks and high-heeled shoes."

He dipped his head, humble as any common church mouse. "But Nanu Nakula lives to serve his lady."

"I do not censure thee, Nanu Nakula. Long wert thou trapped as Beautiful," I said, trying to see things as he had. "Impatience decayed into a foul temper, and so thou took thy revenge by mocking thy young master."

"Thinkest thou so?" the mongoose asked warily.

Winnie had wrinkled her forehead in irritation. "Talk English so I can understand."

I kept my eyes on the mongoose. "We were discussing the nature of wishes, weren't we?"

"Wishing is as noble an art as painting or poetry," the mongoose agreed. "And so is the art of wish giving."

Maybe that was another reason he had brought all that trash to Winnie.

"If wishes are an art form," I asked, "does it offend

you when someone makes an imperfect wish?" He said nothing, but when he shifted uncomfortably from one hind paw to the other, I knew I had hit the mark. "But as a servant, you can hardly complain. Instead, you get even by magnifying the flaws."

"Nanu Nakula is in awe." The mongoose touched the tips of his forepaws to his head and then spread his forelegs in a gesture of humility. "Your great mind understands far more than his small one. He thanks you for taking the time to explain his actions to him."

I'd heard enough. "Winnie, you can't trust him. Change him into Beautiful before he does any more harm."

The mongoose pleaded with Winnie. "Nanu Nakula knows what a kind master you are now. There will be no more tricks. Have faith in me."

"Blow the whistle," I told Winnie.

Winnie cupped both hands defensively around the mongoose. "Everybody deserves a second chance."

I blinked because that's exactly what Caleb said about his charity cases. Of course, none of them could have caused the mischief that this pest could.

I had hoped that meeting Caleb would show Winnie that she could model herself after her kind, courageous great-grandfather rather than her ruthless grandfather Jarvis. So I could hardly complain now if she was demonstrating as tender a heart as Caleb's.

Besides, I was relieved to learn that the mongoose was behind the break-in and the pranks because it meant no real adversary could penetrate my safeguards or eavesdrop on us.

The real threat wasn't a practical joker like the mongoose but a possible villain who had tried to strand Winnie in the past. The lost badge might have been an accident, and it might have been a coincidence that the woman who had shouted "t'ief" had come from Romania, Lady Luminita's homeland—there were fairgoers from around the world after all.

But if some ruthless enemy had tried to strand Winnie in the past, he or she had to be stopped before they could strike again.

So I warned the mongoose in Sanskrit, "Thy master trusts thee, though I know not why. Betray that trust, and I will cause thy fur to fly away like wheat chaff in the wind. And I tell thee, Nanu Nakula, that a bald mongoose is far uglier than a plucked chicken."

He was as slippery with words as he would have been fighting against a cobra. "He will try to recall thy warning, but . . . ," he said, rapping his paw on his skull, "his little head can only hold a few memories."

I pointed a claw at him like a judge sentencing a prisoner. "If thy tiny brain remembers one thing, it must be this: Grief will befall all who cause grief to Winnie."

"What did you say to him?" Winnie demanded suspiciously. "Are you picking on him?"

Since I was trying to protect her, that seemed singularly ungrateful, especially when the mongoose popped up from behind her fingers and smirked at me. "You heard Nanu Nakula's master."

Right then and there, I should have insisted that Winnie transform the mongoose once more into an expensive but harmless trinket. But I didn't consider him as much of a threat as those troublemaking enemies.

I couldn't help wondering if I was making a big mistake. A trickster mongoose loaded with wishes could be more dangerous than a pistol loaded with bullets.

CHAPTER THIRTEEN

Get your wish right the first time.
You may not get a do-over.

MISS DRAKE

After I'd seen Winnie safely at school—Rowan again escorted her—I texted Reynard to see if he had learned anything more about Lady Luminita.

No big deposits in hr bank account. Give me list of yr enemies. Will compare names on yr list to hr recent phone calls & emails.

I started tapping possibilities on my phone . . . and tapping . . . and tapping. When I finally finished, he wrote:

Is that every 1?

Those r just local ones. Complete list will take longer. Much longer.

"So many enemies. Nanu Nakula is impressed." The mongoose was eating the last of my imported coral crackers with the wasabi flavoring. "But maybe next time you should try counting to ten before you lose your temper."

I counted to ten twice before I warned him, "I just did—and it's not working. That was my morning snack."

"Mine too, mine too," he said cheerfully as he brushed the crumbs from his fur. "Have you got any more?"

One bite, I thought. One bite and I can make him disappear. But what would that teach Winnie?

The mongoose saw me grinding my teeth. I suppose he'd become an expert on how far he could pester someone. "Nana Nakula is Helpful. You need him."

"For what?" I sniffed. "I want to stop whoever's threatening Winnie, not rob their house."

"Nanu Nakula can find your enemy. He knows all about feuds," he boasted. "After all, he has started enough of them."

I imagine he had after one rich lady saw another wearing the jewels he had stolen. "Do you ever feel sorry for the misery you've caused?"

He swiped a paw around the plate, trying to pick up any crumbs. "Nanu Nakula does not make the wish. He merely fulfills it. You do not blame a knife when it cuts you instead of your steak, do you?"

I'd seen enough of this pest to know he wasn't blameless. "No doubt you're an expert at nudging your master into making a wish that would do the maximum harm."

He scratched his belly lazily. "Is it Nanu Nakula's fault that his masters always ask for more than they can handle?"

"Humans live such short lives that they have to stretch for things way beyond their grasp," I corrected him. "It's ridiculous, but it's also what makes them human. And yes, it often leads them into the silliest messes, but sometimes . . . sometimes they achieve the most glorious things."

It's why I love humans. For all our noble virtues, dragons have such strength and power and live such long lives that everything is in our reach, and no ambition is too outrageous. And so we dragons do not need to dream like humans: we make our thousand-year plans instead.

He sat upon the plate. "How lucky you are. Nanu Nakula only seems to encounter the greedy sort of human."

"Winnie wished for world peace," I countered. "What's greedy about that?"

He folded his legs. "She is young yet."

"She will surprise you," I predicted. She certainly had already amazed me—most of the time in a good way.

Before he could reply, Reynard began typing again:

I will begin checking your local enemies. But mayb
faster 2 search lady's house 4 evidence. Can u get
hr out of hr house 2night?

I reminded Reynard:

She is werewolf.

No problem. Wil bring doggy treats.

Reynard was quite the fearless fellow when he wasn't infatuated with movie celebrities, and I blessed my stars that he was my friend. I answered:

Then I called Willamar. "I know who stole the Heart of Kubera."

"Who?! How?!" Willamar asked, too excited to be his usual formal self.

"All will soon be revealed," I said coyly. "Can you call a special meeting for tonight at seven and make sure the whole club is there?"

"You couldn't keep them away with an army, especially Lady Luminita," he assured me, and hung up to begin contacting the other members.

After informing Reynard that I'd arranged for Lady Luminita to be at a meeting at seven, I turned to the mongoose. "Do you mean it when you say you want to be Helpful?"

The mongoose bounced up and down. "Of course, of course."

I looked at him sternly. "Then it's very important you do exactly what your master asks because she's in great danger," I explained.

His paw instinctively scratched his neck. "From the werewolf?"

"Yes," I said. "She will be there along with a lot of other people who will ask you a lot of questions. It's vital to keep them talking to you as long as you can and not pull any tricks."

"Nanu Nakula can do that." He leaned forward as if about to run a race. "But I can also search the werewolf's house right now, and she will never notice."

"I can't tell you what to look for, though," I said, "so we'll stick to my original plan. Will you behave for Winnie's sake?"

"Of course. She is Nanu Nakula's master," the mongoose promised.

He seemed sincere enough, but even if he didn't cooperate, I would be at the meeting too and would give Reynard the time he needed. Reynard had a keen fox's nose for anything that looked or smelled fishy.

That afternoon after school, Rowan was waiting outside for Winnie. Smirking to one another, Winnie's friends made a point of saying loud good-byes to both her and Rowan and then giggled as they walked away. Their reactions definitely did not help her mood.

I hadn't realized Winnie's face could turn such an interesting shade of red. I think she would have hit Rowan with her book bag but didn't want to make even more of a scene. Instead, she stamped off toward home.

With his odd bouncing stride, he easily caught up with her. "How did school go today?"

Winnie didn't answer but looked straight ahead. She had too many bad experiences in past schools, with people trying to befriend her only to betray her. As a Shielder, Rowan could do that anytime.

He seemed determined to strike up a conversation. "We get a lot of homework. What about you?"

Without turning her head, she said, "You don't get much practice with small talk, do you?"

He blinked, his eyes a dusky green as he stared at the odd fingers of his hands and then stuffed them in his pockets. "There aren't many people I want to speak to," he said awkwardly.

Among adult magicals in San Francisco, it has become a rule of etiquette that we don't publicly comment on one another's appearance. After all, to a griffin anyone without wings and a beak would seem odd.

But it's a rule magicals learn the hard way while they grow up and are hurt and hurt in turn. When magicals are young, they are as likely to make fun of anyone different just as young normals would.

Rowan with his odd hands and walk had probably had his share of insults. He might have developed his air of aloofness as a kind of shield to keep people away from him. I wasn't sure why he wanted to drop that shield with Winnie, but I had my suspicions. Unfortunately, he had such little practice chatting with someone, so he was clumsy at it.

Rowan's gnarly fingers and his mysterious eyes, ever-changing like the sea, intrigued me. I had a hunch that Rowan's history began with my friend Gilbert's sadness and loneliness after his son died. Had the wizard created the figure of a boy who resembled his son from things around his beach hideaway—driftwood and sea glass? Had he somehow brought his creation to life? But how had his sea boy become human, like Pinocchio? No matter, it was Rowan's story, and he would have to tell us if and when he chose. Until then, I might buy the boy some shin guards.

He kept up the one-sided conversation all the way to the foot of our driveway, where he stopped. "I'll see you tonight," he said. Apparently, he'd received the same message as the club members about the special meeting tonight.

Winnie ignored him as she nodded to Paradise, who was raking some dead leaves. She dipped her head to Winnie respectfully and then, as I instructed her earlier, called to Rowan. "Mr. Rowan, would you like a cup of tea with the lady of the house?"

Winnie whirled around. "Mother's not home yet."

"The other lady of the house," Paradise explained.

"He's not . . . ," Winnie started to say.

At that moment, Vasilisa opened the front door. "Tea will be ready in a few minutes," she announced. "Won't you come in, Mr. Rowan?"

Winnie looked shocked at her friends' betrayal, and I left them to handle her while I circled around to my apartments. Once again a respectable size, I made my way upstairs and could smell the tea brewing in a pot.

I found Winnie in an easy chair as she glowered at Rowan. Poor boy. He was sitting on the sofa staring at the bay rather than his host.

He didn't seem surprised or frightened to see my true form. Instead, he pointed a twisted finger. "What's that funny spot on your scales?"

There was nothing wrong with his eyes, now emerald green. "It's where I keep my phone," I said, curling up in a chair.

"It could be a weak spot for a bullet," he said.

He had no idea what topics were unsuitable for polite discussion. "No, the real scale is behind the pocket," I said.

He pursed his lips thoughtfully. "Smart."

Winnie couldn't hold her anger in anymore as she

turned to me accusingly. "What's the idea of letting him in our house?"

"Because I wanted to ask for his help again," I said to her, and then faced Rowan. "Did your aunt tell you there was a special meeting of the club tonight?" Even though I knew the answer, I had to ask, or Winnie might have suspected I'd been following her.

"Yes, she received the message this afternoon and passed it on to me," he said. "So you've solved the theft?"

Winnie couldn't resist gloating. "And found the thief."

"Who was it?" Rowan asked.

I held up a claw. "I'm pretty sure you'll meet him soon."

Rowan's eyes widened. "He's still alive?"

"Patience," I instructed him.

A moment later, Vasilisa came in with a tray bearing everything we would need for afternoon tea—frosted cakes, berried scones, and little crustless sandwiches.

No sooner had she set everything down than there was a tan streak and the mongoose was on the table, then on the tray itself. He started to reach for a sandwich but caught sight of a scone as large as himself. He leapt to reach for that when he saw one of Vasilisa's special cookies, but before he could take it, he saw a macaroon that tempted him.

He rubbed his head with both paws in frustration. "Decisions, decisions," he muttered.

Vasilisa picked him up by the back of his neck. "We talked about this already. Guests get served first."

I'm not sure what had happened between them, but when Small Doll rustled in the pocket of Vasilisa's apron, Nanu Nakula grew still and didn't try to protest.

"Yes, yes, guests get served first." He couldn't resist adding with a warning look at Rowan. "Even if they look greedy."

Rowan pointed at the mongoose. "Is that your pet?" he asked Winnie.

Almost at the same time, the mongoose jabbed a claw at Rowan and asked Winnie. "Is he your beau? Your boyfriend?"

"No!" Winnie answered both emphatically.

For a while, all three were silent as they ate. When they had done justice to Vasilisa's offerings, I cleared my throat. "Rowan, I invited you to tea because I'd like to report to you in your official capacity as a Shielder." Though we had solved one mystery, I explained our suspicions about Lady Luminita working for one of my enemies to harm Winnie. "I want to ask the Council not to arrest her until I learn who planned this all. I hope to have evidence soon."

This was all news to Winnie, too, of course. "What will you do if Sir Isaac's recordings show Lady Luminita stayed at the ball?" she asked. "I mean, I know he was concentrating on Lady Gravelston, but maybe he caught Lady Luminita in the background."

"Then that will reduce the suspects by one," I said, "and I will simply start the hunt again."

"If there is a conspiracy against you, it could have changed time itself." Rowan nodded. "I'm sure the Council will want to find the real culprit as much as you do."

"And who's pulling his or her strings," Winnie added.

Rowan glared at her. "There are more polite ways of saying that."

"What's this thing you got against puppets?" Winnie asked.

"Nothing," he said in a firm, flat voice that I suspected he hoped would end her questioning.

Hmmmm. Perhaps it wasn't puppets that made him uncomfortable so much as a puppet maker like Geppetto, but again, this wasn't the time to raise the subject—if ever. "So will you pass this information on to your superiors?"

"Of course," Rowan said.

Winnie and I were ready by 6:40 p.m. I was in my human disguise, but both Winnie and I wore modern clothes this time. The pest was riding in the pocket of her blouse, and the both of them were looking far too comfortable with the arrangement.

"Do you have the whistle?" I whispered.

"Got it." She pointed to the pocket, where it sat next to the mongoose. When we stepped outside, we found Rowan standing alert by the front door.

"You again?" Winnie asked, annoyed.

Rowan shrugged. "I've spoken to the Council, and it's ordered me to accompany you. Also, there will be two gold Shielders dressed as servants at the meeting."

I motioned to the cab by the curb. "And here's our taxi. Excellent timing." But when we reached the sidewalk, Nanu Nakula began to rock frantically in Winnie's pocket, and his fur began to bristle. "Something is wrong. So wrong."

Then Winnie whispered, so the others wouldn't hear, "My ring . . . it's flashing red."

I didn't sense anything myself, but it was better to be safe than sorry. So I put my arm out to block Winnie and noticed Rowan had also slipped in front of her.

The woman cabby tapped the steering wheel impatiently. "Hurry up. I ain't got all day," she said to me, but her eyes were focused on Winnie.

"It must be very busy for you," I said as I studied her. From the waist up, she seemed normal enough, blond hair pulled away from her face, purple sweatshirt with Williams College stenciled on it. From the waist down, though, she held her denim-clad legs tightly together as if they were glued.

"She hasn't blinked her eyes yet," Rowan observed.

"She's a lamia," I said. She was half serpent, so no wonder she had made the mongoose uneasy.

The first lamia had been placed under a horrid curse where she could not close her eyes while she saw the faces of her dead children. And yet she must have had more daughters afterward because the shape and the stare had been passed on to her descendants. She probably had been staring at the enemy of serpents, the mongoose, rather than Winnie.

"Winnie, hold on to the mongoose and get inside the house," I ordered, preparing to do battle.

"Well, aren't you the clever wormy," the lamia said, and pulled a lever on the dashboard.

The trunk lid popped up and out rolled kobolds, small squat creatures with hair that bristled like old toothbrushes and large-eared heads on thin necks. They burned easily in the sun, so they wore an assortment of caps and sunglasses that made them look like strange little tourists—except for the short pickaxes on their belts. Kobolds used them for fighting as well as mining, so I knew they meant business. Lady Luminita must be feeling desperate to try to kidnap us where anyone could spot us.

There was no time to worry about the neighbors seeing my true form. I had to become a dragon to protect Winnie, so I moved my hands and muttered the spell.

When the golden haze began to dissipate, I got ready to knock the kobolds into the street, but with a grin, the lamia flung a long strip of yellow paper at me.

"Nighty night," she called.

The paper flew straight as an arrow, and I glimpsed the enchanted symbols written in bright red ink that told me it was a magical charm. I started to duck but too late.

The paper flattened tight against my shoulder, and I heard Winnie shout, "Miss Drake!"

And then the world went black.

CHAPTER FOURTEEN

Above all, be careful what you wish for.

⤳ Winnie ⤳

Sss. Sss. Sss . . . I heard a sound like a file on an old, rusty nail.

"Wake up!" a harsh voice said.

The cement floor was cold, and the dusty air smelled like old rotting magazines. The last thing I remembered was Miss Drake falling on the sidewalk and the mongoose leaving me. Then Rowan shouted that we had to get the charm off.

We both tried to rip the charm away at the same time, but blue light crackled and twisted like snakes around our hands. That was the last thing I remembered.

I was laying on my side now. My hip hurt where it pressed against the concrete, and my shoulders ached from having my arms pulled behind me. There was something tight around my wrists and also around my ankles, so I figured that I must have been tied up. I couldn't see my ring, but I'm sure it was still flashing red—flashing with the beating of my racing heart.

My toes felt cold, which made me realize I didn't have my shoes on anymore.

When I raised my eyelids, I saw the cabby. She'd changed from her sweatshirt into a pullover blouse with purple sequins. From the waist down, she was a serpent with violet scales that matched her blouse.

Behind her, next to a very tall candelabra with six candles, my shoes were lying in tatters, so she must have been searching for something hidden inside or in the heel. Rowan's pair must have been the black ones, also torn up, that lay a foot beyond mine.

"The wormy said she had solved the theft," the lamia said. "So you must know about the whistle. What happened to it? Where is it?"

About twenty feet away, I saw a large circle of light

made by a ring of more candelabra shining on Miss Drake's scales. The yellow strip of paper on her shoulder gleamed against her scales.

She was lying so still. Was she dead? I breathed a sigh of relief when I saw her chest rise. She was still breathing but slowly, like she was in a deep sleep.

Five kobolds were poking and prodding her. I wanted to shout at them to stop it because I knew how much she would have hated that.

"Ansssswer me!" the lamia hissed, sounding annoyed now. "Where isss the whissstle?"

The ivory whistle had been in my blouse pocket, but I couldn't feel it anymore. And there was no sign of Nanu Nakula either. Maybe when he saw Miss Drake being kidnapped, he'd taken the whistle and hid.

But I played dumb. "What whistle?"

I tensed when she raised a hand to slap me, but Rowan said, "Don't you dare hit her!"

With a snarl, the lamia jerked her head at Rowan. "You're my prisssonersss. I want the whissstle."

Rowan didn't have to pretend to be ignorant. "I don't know anything about a whistle."

A cell phone buzzed, and the lamia answered it, her voice calm and controlled again. "Yes, we've searched them." I assume she was speaking to Lady Luminita, who was probably at the meeting so no one would suspect she was behind the kidnapping. But she must have slipped outside to check on her servants' progress. The lamia's voice grew exasperated. "None of them has the whistle. And the brats claim they know nothing. They look pretty stupid, so they probably don't."

I didn't like the way the lamia grinned. "With pleasure, master," she said, and put her phone away before she clicked her fingers at a kobold guarding a heavy wooden door. "Bring me the magical charms."

The kobold opened the doors and disappeared into the shadows while the lamia slithered toward Miss Drake. Her dry scales rippled over the floor, and I heard again: *Sss. Sss. Sss.*

I looked around the windowless rock walls. The stones looked old and dirty, and there were patches of green stuff growing on the mortar. Then I heard the faint sound of rushing water like a toilet had broken. "Where are we?" I whispered to Rowan.

"I think we're in the basement of an old house," he said. "When San Francisco expanded, they just covered over a lot of little creeks. I think there's one on the other side of the wall."

Suddenly a tan streak zipped through the open door toward me. The next moment I felt the mongoose's breath tickle my ear. "When Nanu Nakula saw the Snake Lady, he knew she wanted him and the whistle, so he escaped. And when they captured you, he followed them. Is Nanu Nakula not faithful?"

I'm glad I'd trusted him instead of listening to Miss Drake. "You're the faithfullest," I said softly. "And the whistle?"

"Well hidden," the mongoose said.

"You are the smartest," I said approvingly. "Now get these cords off me."

"Nanu Nakula is sorry. You must make a wish, not a command," the mongoose corrected me. "Those are the rules. But remember, be careful how you wish."

Why didn't magic work like it did in the stories? In the fairy tales, you just pick up an old brass lamp and rub it and presto! You've got a genie who will do anything you want. Not a mongoose with a rule book. But he had made me think about wishes. How wishes in books like *Five Children and It* could go very wrong if you weren't careful. So, I told myself, think before you make a wish . . . if you ever got a chance to make your wishes count again.

The kobold who had left stumped back. I expected the magical charms to be in some ancient carved wooden chest, but he was carrying a black binder—the kind like you kept schoolwork in. I suppose it was cheaper and more practical than something more impressive and mystical.

The kobold headed toward the lamia, and I whispered, "Okay." Rewording everything made it more complicated. "I wish for the cords tying my hands and feet, but they must be off my wrists and ankles and in my hands instead."

"Then the cords you shall have." I felt the mongoose tug and gnaw at the cords around my wrists. The munching sounds seemed loud to me, but the lamia was too busy leafing through the binder pages, each of which was like a transparent pocket. She looked like a collector going through her stamp collection. Instead of stamps, there were more yellow strips of paper with writing on them. Each pocket must have had a label because her lips moved as she read it. And in their little grating voices, all the kobolds were busy making suggestions about which charm to use.

As soon as the cords around my wrists dropped off, the mongoose began to work on the cords around my ankles. My hands and feet felt funny as the blood rushed into them again, but I felt the pieces of cut cord in my palm. He'd kept his word after all without any tricks.

"Is Nanu Nakula not Helpful?" he asked, fishing for another compliment.

"Yes, you are," I agreed. "Now I wish for the cords tying up Rowan."

"Then his cords you shall have," the mongoose said.

There were munching sounds, and I glanced at the lamia and the kobolds to see if they'd noticed, but they were still too busy arguing over spells.

"Here it is," the lamia grunted. "Something to wake the wormy up that will let her talk but not let her make trouble."

The tip of the paper wriggled like a serpent hunting for a tasty meal. With a grin, the lamia let it go, and the new charm fastened itself to the scales of Miss Drake's chest.

Then the lamia reached for the one attached to Miss Drake. Blue electricity crackled, and the lamia's face twisted in pain until she was able to wriggle backward, sucking on her burnt fingers.

The kobolds started to jeer, and one of them pointed a long knobby arm at the snake woman. "Stupid, Stupid! You forgot the charm was protected."

"Shut up."

The lamia swatted at the kobold, who bent his head so that her hand hit the top of his hard skull. *"Ow, ow, ow."*

When I felt Rowan's cords in my palm too, I made sure to tell the mongoose, "Thank you."

He spoke slowly, as if in wonder. "No one has ever thanked Nanu Nakula in all these thousands of years."

"No one?" Poor little guy. I guess his other owners had ignored the fact that he was a living, breathing someone and treated him instead like a magical ATM machine: push the button and out comes money. No wonder he had made their wishes go wrong if he could. "Well, they should have," I said firmly.

Rowan rustled to get my attention. "We can't take them on by ourselves. We should sneak away and get help."

I didn't like the idea of my dragon lying helpless with an angry snake woman and kobolds around. "I'm not leaving without Miss Drake. Let me think of something."

There was a red cord hanging from the binder, which I thought helped mark a place in it, but the lamia pulled the cord free. At one end hung a gold oval, which she touched to the first charm on Miss Drake. The paper instantly disintegrated into powder.

The next moment, Miss Drake blinked groggily. The oval had deactivated the charm.

The lamia tucked the gold oval and cord into her breast pocket and then spoke slowly, exaggerating each syllable. "Worm! Where . . . is . . . the . . . whistle?"

Miss Drake didn't answer. Instead, she tried to get

up, but her body barely shifted. Her eyes could move, though, and she glanced at me. I took a chance and gave her a thumbs-up.

Reassured, she became her usual cranky self and glared at the lamia. "What's so important about a whistle? Shouldn't you be looking for the Heart of Kubera?"

The lamia threw the binder down on the floor with a thump. Miss Drake had a real talent for making everyone lose their tempers. And when the lamia got angry, her narrow forked tongue darted out more, making her hiss her words. "The Heart belongsss to the one with the whissstle. And the whissstle belongsss to my massster. A human brat ssstole it from my massster'sss grandfather a hundred yearsss ago before he could ussse it."

I thought about the desperate kiosk owner who had tried to get the whistle from my great-granddad Caleb. Who could be the man's grandchild?

"On the contrary, I saw the child pay money for it," Miss Drake argued. "Your master has no claim on it."

The lamia's mouth twisted into the scowl of all scowls and hissed, "You have it now. You called a meeting to show the jewel and the whissstle to everyone and gloat."

Miss Drake gave the lamia her haughtiest stare. "I merely solved a hundred-year-old mystery. I didn't say I

184

had the Heart of Kubera itself, let alone some child's toy. You must have searched me. If I had either of them, why didn't you find it?"

"Because you hid it sssomewhere firssst," the lamia argued. "Or sssomeone elssse isss holding it for you."

"I simply ran across a few clues in old books and connected them together," Miss Drake insisted.

As the lamia continued to argue with Miss Drake, I didn't think Rowan and I could take the snake woman and the kobolds by ourselves.

Finally, I had it. "Nanu Nakula," I called softly.

He was by my ear again. "Yes, master? We can go now?"

"Do you see that binder? It's like a big black book," I asked.

"Yes, master," the mongoose said expectantly.

I thought a moment, trying to make my wish perfect. "I wish for the book. And I wish for only that book and not any others, and I want everything in that book. And when you get it, I wish it was placed behind me where the lamia and kobolds can't see it."

"Of course, master," the mongoose said.

There was a rush of air as he darted toward the lamia and a second breeze when he returned. I felt the binder's hard edges against my spine. My heart began to race.

"Is Nanu Nakula not quick? Is he not strong?" the mongoose wanted to know.

The mongoose needed flattery as much as he wanted snacks. "You're certainly the quickest and strongest. I'm so glad I met you."

"Of course, of course." He was almost preening.

"Now, Nanu Nakula, do you see the red cord in the lamia's pocket?" I asked as sweetly as I could.

"My eyes are the sharpest, master. I see the Snake Lady has it," the mongoose said with a snarl.

"Well, at the end of the cord is a gold token," I said, trying to pin him down on what I wanted him to take.

The mongoose's eyes gleamed. "I know where there's lots more gold."

"I bet you do," I said. "But I wish for the cord and the token."

He liked the idea. "Ah, steal from the Snake Lady." His whole body went rigid for a moment.

By now, Miss Drake had made the lamia so mad that she was practically screeching and the kobolds were stamping their feet angrily, sounding like a mini rockslide. They were working themselves into a mood where they could hurt my dragon.

None of them noticed the tan blur that climbed the lamia's scales and onto her blouse. A second later, none of them saw him take the cord and token. And a millisecond after that, not one of them witnessed the mongoose return and put it in my hand.

Rowan murmured, "Okay. Now what?"

"We're going to free Miss Drake." I closed my fingers tightly around the token. "I'm going to count to ten, Rowan. When I reach ten, we're going to sit up and you're going to start pulling charms from the binder and throwing them at the lamia and her gang."

"Without knowing what they are?" he asked skeptically.

"There won't be time to pick and choose," I said to him. "Use whatever you can grab. We just want to confuse 'em."

"And what will you be doing?" Rowan asked.

I was so scared my mouth felt dry. "I'm going to free her with the token."

The mongoose grabbed my sleeve and tugged. "No, no. It's much too dangerous. Run away with Nanu Nakula, and he will grant all your wishes without any tricks."

I gently shoved his paws away. "All I want is my dragon."

"Then a dragon you shall have," Nanu Nakula declared. The next moment, the token was gone from my hand and he was shooting like a furry bolt of lightning toward Miss Drake.

....

⌐∾ MISS DRAKE ∾⌐

When Winnie signed to me that she was all right and I saw the mongoose, I assumed he had freed her as well as Rowan. I kept stalling, waiting for them to sneak away and get help, but Winnie could no more desert me than Caleb could have.

Instead of fleeing, she had the mongoose fetch the black binder. Then, jumping to their feet, Winnie and Rowan began grabbing charms at random from the book and flinging them toward the kobolds and snake woman. Some sailed past to glue themselves to the wall, turning one spot puce and making another drip with molasses. Others clung to the kobolds. One of them had his arm swell up. Another began warbling like a bird. Still another turned into a gingerbread kobold complete with frosting.

The charm that smacked against the snake woman made her shrink to about a yard high, half her size. She slid sideways, shaking in shock.

The hatchlings had confused our enemies. Now was the time for them to escape, but instead they kept throwing more charms.

"Get out of here," I ordered them, but they were just as single-minded as the mongoose.

A kobold finally turned with a grunt and began to stumble toward the hatchlings. Two charms hit him at once, and the combination made him swell up like a balloon and float up and up till he grated against the ceiling.

While the lamia and kobolds were distracted, the mongoose suddenly appeared on my shoulder next to the charm immobilizing me. He was holding a token on a red cord in his mouth. When he took it in his forepaws, he whispered in Sanskrit, "This will turn the charm that binds thee into powder. Nanu Nakul does not like thee, but the One with Great Spirit loves thee and so for her sake, he will save thee."

But before he could act, a narrow forked tongue flicked between the lamia's lips as if testing the air. Sensing the mongoose, her body whipped around. Like a snake, she unhinged her jaw so that her human mouth and lips stretched wider and wider—large enough to swallow a cat whole, let alone a tiny mongoose.

The mongoose instinctively became focused on her, his every muscle, every hair, taut and ready. Instantly, he leapt from me to the floor and faced the lamia who, though reduced in size, still towered over her tiny foe.

When she lunged, he hopped nimbly to the side and then struck.

With a cry, the lamia straightened up as the mongoose sank his teeth into her earlobe. Her tail lashed the floor as she tried to grab him. But bracing his hind legs against her jaw, he somersaulted backward on to her shoulder and then leapt for the side of her throat where the main artery was.

As small as he was, I might have given him even odds of winning if he could have used all four paws, but as it was, he insisted on keeping the token in his forepaws while he fought his uneven battle.

Sensing his goal, the lamia desperately whipped her body back and forth, and the mongoose couldn't keep his grip on her blouse. He flew off and slammed against the wall, where he lay as still as death.

The lamia snatched the token from the floor, and tossing it into her stretched mouth, she swallowed it. Then her dagger-thin tongue stabbed repeatedly as she slithered toward her mortal enemy, the mongoose. "I prefer my mealsss kicking and sssquealing, but I'm willing to make exceptionsss."

Like her, I thought he was unconscious and helpless.

But, like a possum, the mongoose had only been pretending to be unconscious. Waiting until her hands were only inches away, he bounced onto her arm and then ran up it.

"I will do the kicking and you can do the squealing," he taunted, and hit her with his hind paw several times.

He was game for a fight all right, but nursing an injured forepaw against his chest robbed him of his usual speed and grace. Her slap swept him from her arm and arching through the air to fall onto my chest.

He raised his head groggily and struggled up on three paws. "Protect Nanu Nakula's master."

His good paw reached for the paper, but as soon as his claws touched it, tentacles of blue light began to twist around the mongoose and me. I stifled a cry, but my pain must have been nothing compared to the torture his little body was feeling. Yet he only gritted his teeth and kept tugging at the charm even when the tips of his bristling fur began to smoke and a ball of blue light surrounded him.

"Ssstop that," the lamia commanded, her body bobbing up and down and round and round, but not daring to touch the mongoose while the painful glow surrounded him.

When I heard the tearing sound, I saw the mongoose

stagger backward. His fur was burnt, but he triumphantly held up the little patch of paper he had ripped from the charm. The next moment, the lamia's hand threw him against the wall again. Was he faking a second time? Or was he really unconscious?

Though the torn piece was no bigger than a stamp, perhaps it would weaken the charm enough.

I tried to sit up. My body felt like it weighed tons, but I strained every muscle and slowly I began to rise. And the further I stretched, the more bits of the charm began to flake off me and the easier it became to move.

With a screech, the lamia lunged at me, but I swung my paw, clubbing her to the side.

Then I showed my fangs. "In India, I liked to snack on poisonous cobras, and I haven't had snake for ever so long."

On her belly, the frightened lamia wriggled sideways, but I crept on all fours after her, feeling stronger by the second.

She would learn what happened to someone who kidnapped a dragon and her pet.

Chapter Fifteen

*Greedy wishes make no one happy . . .
least of all the wisher.*

Winnie

With a lunge, Miss Drake grabbed the lamia's throat in her right paw and the tail in the other. Then she yanked the snake woman into the air, holding her like a piece of taffy. The kobolds kept drumming their feet against the floor and waving their little pickaxes angrily, trying to work up enough nerve to charge. The dragon's armored scales were tough, but could they stand up to the kobold's tools that smashed through boulders?

As if I'd let that happen!

When I had grabbed the first charm in the binder, Rowan tried to stop me. "Don't fool around with magic. We've been lucky so far but—"

"I'm not going to stand around while they thump Miss Drake," I stated, and threw it.

When it slapped against a kobold's back, he twisted and turned trying to tear it off. He stopped as he began to grow taller and bigger until his head brushed the ceiling, till plaster dust fell.

"Uh-oh," I said. To give Rowan credit, he didn't waste time saying, "I told you so." Instead, he stepped in front of me.

"Find a shrinking spell," he said, and then ran at the kobold waving his arms and making faces. "Hey, ugly!"

The kobold ground his teeth together and swung his arm. It made a loud swishing noise like the wind roaring through a tree.

When Rowan bent his knees, I thought he was starting to duck, but instead, his long, odd toes bent like springs. He shot into the air like he had rockets strapped to his ankles. His long twisty fingers reached and clasped like iron bracelets around the kobold's wrist, and then he swung his body up and wound his legs around the kobold's arm too.

The kobold stood still, puzzled, and began trying to shake Rowan off him.

"H-h-hurry!" Rowan yelled to me as he whipped through the air.

I started searching through the binder's pages, but the labels were hard to read in the candlelight and they just seemed to have been stuck into the binder at random. Nothing made sense and to make things worse, I saw my ring pulsing even faster . . . a brilliant crimson. Then it turned a steady dazzling red . . . which would have been awesome if I didn't suspect it was the gravest warning ever.

"Idiots! I said to keep them quiet until I returned," a woman said in disgust from the doorway. But it wasn't Lady Luminita or Silana . . .

It was Lorelei! Except she wasn't Lorelei either. She was dressed simply but more stylish than before. Her shoulders weren't hunched, and she was holding her head up high with pride. Instead of the timid, mousy woman I'd met at the party, she was a confident warrior.

Lifting her leg, she placed her foot on the side of the nearest kobold and shoved. He stumbled right into me, and I dropped the binder. As we fell to the floor together, he wrapped his arms around my body. He smelled of rotten eggs like that experiment Sir Isaac had done with sulfur last week. Then he rolled onto his back, so I had to face Lorelei.

She picked up her binder. "Now, Miss Drake, put down that idiot."

Instead, Miss Drake held the lamia in front of her. "I'll trade you. Your right-hand monster for the two hatchlings."

The lamia's forked tongue lashed the air frantically. "Pleassse, massster."

Lorelei began to leaf through her binder, frowning when she saw how many pockets Rowan and I had emptied. "Do what you want with her, Miss Drake. You'll spare me the chore of getting rid of her."

Miss Drake tapped the lamia's head against the wall, and then she set the unconscious snake woman down on the floor. "I thought the kobolds looked familiar—only the last time I saw them, there was a drought demon in charge. So you got rid of him?"

Lorelei sniffed contemptuously. "Permanently. Clipper had a gem I wanted, and he was supposed to get it cheap. Instead, thanks to you, he returned with nothing." She slipped two charms from the binder.

Miss Drake's hind paw shoved the sleeping lamia to the side and started to advance. "Let Winnie go."

Lorelei tossed one of the charms against the floor, where it burst into flames, and she then held its twin over me. "Stop where you are, Miss Drake, or I'll reduce this pest to ash."

Miss Drake froze in place. "You're a regular Dr. Jekyll and Ms. Hyde, aren't you? Meek to some people and mean to others."

I remembered watching a movie once where a scientist had come up with a potion that changed him into a monster. I don't know what happened after that because Dad had come into the room and turned off the television. But I don't think the movie monster could have been scarier than Lorelei.

Lorelei curtsied. "Why, thank you. Good reviews are always appreciated." Then she bent her head and hunched her shoulders like the party wallflower she'd pretended to be. "I've picked up a few tricks acting and singing in dinner theater and touring companies." She slipped into Lady Luminita's accent. "And for an act in Vegas, I learned to imitate almost anybody's voice."

"But why try to strand Winnie in the past?" Miss Drake demanded. "That was beyond cruel."

Straightening up, she glared at me. "Because she was cruel to me."

"What did I do?" I said. I don't think I'd even talked to her.

She thrust her head forward. "You yawned! That's the worst thing you can do to a performer. I've put up with humiliations like that for years, but once I found the box with my grandfather's charms, I knew I didn't have to put up with insults any longer."

"No, the worst that can happen to a performer is when Ivan the Terrible doesn't understand your joke and orders your head cut off because a shorter jester might be funnier," Miss Drake said. "Anyway, when did you have time to plot your revenge on Winnie?"

"I was originally going to pick my victim at random." Lorelei shrugged. "I knew the date and time and place when my grandfather lost the whistle, so I took off my badge and slipped away from the ball and made myself invisible. I planned to pick the nearest fairgoer and make it look like that person had stolen the purse. Then while everyone was distracted, I would have grabbed the whistle from the brat who had it. But when I saw Winnie, I decided a little payback was in order. Two birds with one stone, you see."

"I didn't mean to be rude," I said. "I was tired."

Miss Drake shrugged. "But even if she had intended to be rude, the punishment hardly fit the crime."

"I've got the power now. *I decide* what's fitting and what's not," Lorelei screeched, and jerked her head at the giant kobold who was standing ten feet away with Rowan still holding on to him. "You, tall and gruesome, lower your arm." She shut her eyes in exasperation when he put down his free hand. "Not that arm! The one with the brat attached to it." When he did, she jerked her head at a pair of the regular-size kobolds. "You two paperweights. Douse the fire and then pull the pest off and hold on to him."

While the pair obeyed Lorelei, I heard the *click-click-click* of little claws on cement as the mongoose limped toward me. I almost cried when I saw how much of his fur was singed.

He'd gotten hurt trying to fulfill my wish, but he didn't seem to hold a grudge. Instead, he tried to free me by pulling at the arm of the kobold that was imprisoning me. "Unh. Uh," he grunted. But he might as well have been tugging at a mountain.

Lorelei swung around. "Is this the Heart of Kubera?" she asked in a hushed voice.

"You know about his two forms?" Miss Drake asked.

"My grandfather spent years piecing the story together, and just when he had bought the whistle, that boy cheated him of his destiny."

I didn't think it was smart right then to mention that the "boy" had been my great-granddad Caleb.

"But when I heard about the Fellowship of the Jewel City," Lorelei went on, "I realized it was my chance to recover my grandfather's whistle. I talked that fool Willamar into organizing the trip for a certain date in the past. And the purse snatching worked perfectly but the boy disappeared before I could get to him."

"So you caused all that trouble for nothing," Miss Drake said.

"I thought I'd lost the whistle just like my grandfather had," Lorelei said smugly, "but then Willamar called the special meeting and said you had solved it."

"Let go of my master!" The mongoose bared his teeth, and I felt his hind paws tense for a leap at Lorelei.

"Don't attack her!" I said to the mongoose. "You might make her drop the charm on me by accident."

Lorelei glared at me contemptuously. "I don't know what kind of trick you're trying to pull by pretending to be the master. Miss Drake would never let a twit like you keep the whistle and all that power."

The mongoose growled, "She is the best and only master."

Lorelei didn't want to believe anything good about me. Dangling the fire charm over me, she sneered, "I dare you to prove it."

I had to turn the tables on her. I needed one wish:

the right wish, a perfectly clear wish the mongoose would grant. But what?

I dipped my head, trying to think, and I caught sight of my ring. The gem was still glowing red, but now there was a bright golden spark in the center, twirling until it took the shape of something. A dagger . . . a ship . . . no, a bird with wings outstretched. A golden eagle!

I had my answer. I knew my wish. But I couldn't spring my trap while a twitch of Lorelei's fingers could turn me into a fireball.

I tilted my head to look at the mongoose. The little black beads of his eyes looked alive and sharp and eager to please. But was he intelligent enough to understand what I wanted? I had to wait for her to move the charm away from me before I could find out.

So I acted like she'd scared me into cooperating. It wasn't too hard to look frightened. She was holding the fire charm between just her index finger and thumb, and her grip didn't look all that tight. "Please don't hurt me. What do you want? A purse full of gold?"

"A small mind thinks small." Lorelei laughed scornfully. "Bring me gold. Lots and lots of gold."

"Do you have anything to heal my servant?" I asked. "It will go a lot faster if he can use all four paws."

"Can't he heal himself?" Lorelei asked.

I guess her grandfather's research hadn't been that complete after all. "He can only bring you things that he can pick up in his paws," I said.

I was hoping she'd need both hands to handle the binder—in which case, I'd make the perfect wish that would fix her wagon. But to my disappointment, she set the binder on the floor and used her left hand to select a charm. And during all that, her right hand continued to hold the fire charm over me.

She dropped the healing charm over the mongoose and it clung to him so I could see his shape under the paper. Then the charm just seemed to melt into his fur. It was still singed, but he wriggled each of his four paws one by one.

"I can run again; I can dance." And to celebrate, Nanu swung in a circle, becoming a tan blur for a moment before stopping again.

Lorelei tapped her foot impatiently. "I'm waiting."

Okay. Stall for more time until she gets careless.

Even though I thought I could trust him now, I didn't want to take a chance he would misunderstand me—not with the fire charm hanging over me. "Bring me oodles of twenty-dollar gold American coins, the kind with eagles on them," I said to the mongoose. A former boss of Mom's had one he kept for luck.

"Then gold coins you shall have," the mongoose said, and streaked from the room.

A few minutes later, there were heaps and heaps of gold coins around me—it was anyone's guess where the mongoose had stolen them. For his own amusement, he had added other solid gold treasures he had swiped as well.

"There." He spread his forepaws as he looked up at Lorelei. "This proves she is my one, true and only master."

Rowan gasped, and the kobolds edged toward the gold with greedy smiles, fingers twitching eagerly to snatch it up.

"Thank you," I said as he scampered over to me and leaned his head against my trapped arm.

"In all the centuries, I have only had one master who thanked me," he said.

Despite all the gold shining around us, Lorelei was still reluctant to say anything positive about me. "You may be the master, but you still think too small."

Here it comes. Time to spring the trap. "Would you like more gold?" I coaxed.

"Fool!" Lorelei jabbed the fire charm down at me like a knife. "Do you really think I'd settle for another wish when I can have the whistle and all the wishes I want?"

The mongoose began bobbing up and down in alarm. "No, no, do not give her the power over me," he begged.

I should have figured this would happen: of course Lorelei would want to become the master. But then I saw how I could still make this work.

"Bring me the whistle," I said, trying to hint to him that I wanted him to find the flaws in her wishes. "And when I give it to Lorelei, I want you to treat her wishes with as much respect as you did mine when we first met."

The mongoose's head jerked up like he suspected what I was up to. He really was a smart little guy.

"Ah!" The mongoose dipped his head humbly. "Then one whistle you shall have, master."

He zipped off and returned with the whistle clenched in his mouth. His back was to Lorelei so she couldn't see him wink before he set it down on top of me. Then he stroked my cheek with his muzzle, stopping long enough by my ear to whisper so faintly only I could hear him, "Trust me, O cleverest of masters."

Lorelei snatched up the ancient ivory whistle and turned it over and over in her left hand. "Yes, that's just how grandfather described it." She raised it over her head in triumph. "I've got it! I've got it!" She danced away from the binder and around the basement, waving the whistle in one hand and the fire charm in the other. "Oh, Grandfather, if you could only see me now!"

"You've got what you want," Miss Drake said. "Now let us go."

Lorelei signed to the kobolds to free Rowan and me. Immediately, Miss Drake gathered us together, folding her wings around us like shields. "And now we'll take our leave."

"You're not going anywhere." Lorelei pointed the fire charm at us like a pistol. "You still haven't paid for all the trouble and grief that you've caused me."

Flames didn't scare a dragon. Bending her long neck, Miss Drake whispered into our ears, "Get ready to run. I'll hold them off."

The mongoose had said to trust him so I would. "No, wait."

Lorelei held the whistle in the crook of her arm like it was a scepter as she gazed down at the mongoose. "Who is your master?" she demanded.

The mongoose bent his head humbly. "You are."

"Then bring me more gold coins like these," she commanded.

The mongoose spread his paws to indicate the heaps of gold eagles carpeting the floor. "But, master, coins are so boring when there is so much lovely other gold in the world."

I tried to nudge Lorelei into making an apparently perfect but imperfect wish. "Lorelei, don't you mean all kinds of gold?"

Lorelei's eyes got dreamy for a moment. I bet she was picturing herself wearing gold jewelry from head to toe— crowns, necklaces, bracelets, and rings studded with gems on every finger. "Yes, yes." She waved the whistle above her head like a conductor's baton. "Cover me in anything gold."

With a bow, the mongoose announced, "If gold is what you want, then gold you shall have!"

And the next moment he was gone.

Chapter Sixteen

⚬৩৬⚬

The three rules of wishing are these:
wish well, wish wisely, and then stop before
you turn into a fool . . . or a goose.

⚬ MISS DRAKE ⚬

When Winnie told me to wait, I
knew my pet must be up to
something, though I didn't know
what. But she'd already proven
on our other adventures
that I could trust her.
My pet was almost bold
and clever enough to be
a dragon. So I simply
watched the gold coins

gather higher and higher around Lorelei's ankles while the mongoose streaked here and there.

Laughing, Lorelei stooped to scoop up some in her hands. She immediately looked puzzled, though, and when she dropped them, they didn't clink.

When the tan blur entered the room, she scowled at the mongoose. "I don't want candy in gold foil. I want real gold."

The mongoose scampered up her leg and was on her shoulder before she could even begin to wiggle. When she turned her astonished head to look at him, he bowed neatly. "Then real gold you shall have."

He was gone in the blink of an eye. "As long as you know who's m-m-master." The blur returned, and the next moment her eyebrows stretched all way up to her hairline and her eyeballs bulged.

"Ooh!" she said, giving a little hop. "Ooh!"

Suddenly her shoes skidded on the candy underfoot, and she fell to the floor. "Get them away! Get them away!" she screamed.

The kobolds, though, stayed where they were, too scared to get near the things wriggling inside her dress. The only one who wasn't afraid to approach was the mongoose, who was moving so fast now I barely glimpsed the tan lightning. But in barely a minute, there were dozens of things squirming under her clothes.

When I heard the faint plop, at first, I thought it was a drop of water from a leaking pipe. But then I saw the goldfish flapping on top of the candy. I watched a second slide out of her sleeve to join the first.

"Do you not like real goldfish, master?" the mongoose asked, and didn't wait for an answer. "Then I shall bring you more real gold." And he streaked off.

Lorelei's hair hung down around her face in a tangle, making her look wild and crazy. "Make that little rat stop," she snarled at us.

Winnie nodded to the whistle in her other hand. "I'm not his master anymore, remember?"

Lorelei looked even more furious as she rose on her knees, but before she could say anything, her face disappeared behind a cascade of what first appeared as bouncing lemons but turned into a lively flock of bright yellow goldfinches. They twittered cheerfully as they flew in artful circles around her head. She tried to hit them with the whistle, but the little acrobats managed to evade it as they continued to spin around her.

"Help—" she began, but then made gagging noises.

She started to get up, and her head momentarily appeared from out of the fuzzy yellow cloud like a mountain peak. Ignoring the fish that now rained down from her clothes, she made spluttering noises before she finally spat out the feathers and then glared at the kobolds.

209

"Help me, you foo—" She resumed choking as the flapping birds swept up to surround her head again.

Realizing that the goldfish weren't that dangerous, the kobolds stomped over and began to wave their arms, eventually driving the birds up to the chandelier, where they perched and chattered gaily to one another as if nothing was unusual.

By then, all the goldfish were out of her dress, but damp golden feathers dotted her hair instead. "What's going on?" Confused and angry, Lorelei stared down at the large bowl in which all the goldfish now swam, thanks to the thoughtful mongoose.

She had just gotten to her feet when the first sheet of music sailed in and hit her arm. It fluttered to the floor, and I saw the title "Silver Threads Among the Gold." Soon there were hundreds of sheet music whirling through the air and striking her. There must have been fifty pounds of them. The ones I glimpsed had *gold* in the name.

"Stop, stop!" she shouted. "I order you to stop!"

But the mongoose was moving so quickly, he was invisible. There was only a series of little booms to mark where he had been. At first, I thought they were explosions, and then I realized the noise was made each time he broke the sound barrier. By racing faster than the speed of sound, he literally outran her commands to halt her wish. What a clever trickster Nanu Nakula could be! Thank heavens!

Thousands of postcards of Golden Gate Park and the Golden Gate Bridge fluttered down on the heap around Lorelei's knees. Miniature souvenir bridges and snow globes began to pile up around her waist, mixing with stuffed animals like golden retrievers and golden monkeys from every toy store in the city.

She tried to stumble away, but by then, the mound of objects covered her to her stomach and her legs were trapped by all the debris. All she could do was stand there helplessly as bright yellow flowers quickly began to pile up toward her chest, hiding all the other golden objects. I had no idea where the mongoose had found that much goldenrod, since it wasn't the season for it.

"Ah-choo!"

Even better, Lorelei was allergic to it.

Her weeping eyes started to widen in panic as she understood that her golden wish was going to suffocate her.

Rowan timed his leap for one of her sneezes, waiting for her eyes to close before he sprang from beneath my wing and grabbed the whistle from Lorelei's hand.

"Give me that!" Lorelei could still move her arms, and she raised the fire charm threateningly.

But Rowan had already jumped back to Winnie and

me, and I could wrap my wing protectively around him again.

"I believe this belongs to you," Rowan said, handing the whistle to Winnie.

It must have infuriated Lorelei to gain her dream, only to lose it again. But her desire for revenge was so overwhelming that she forgot Winnie now had the whistle. Lorelei threw the fire charm at us.

I swung my wing over the hatchlings just in time. When the charm hit it, the flames slid harmlessly across my hide and then instantly died, but some sparks must have landed on the old sheet music and postcards and the paper caught fire. The flowers, which weren't as dry, started to smolder and smoke, and chocolate began to run from the candy coins.

Lorelei flailed her arms. "Save me!"

"Be so kind as to bring me the binder," I told Rowan.

The boy accomplished that with a leap forward and then backward. A quick look at the binder told me that the charms weren't organized by the alphabet or theme or type. On a hunch, my claw flipped to the thickest pages. As I had suspected, Lorelei arranged her charms by the ones she was most likely to use, and I quickly found enough sleep charms to give an army nightmares.

I threw the first of the sleep charms, and it flew straight

as an arrow toward her. She was struggling to extricate herself from the pile of golden objects that were now up to her neck, but as soon as the charm clung to her, she fell asleep standing up.

The sight sent the kobolds stampeding toward the door, and if they hadn't all tried to run through at the same time, they might have escaped. Instead, they jammed together in a grunting, angry knot by the doorway. One by one, I put them to sleep so that they began snoring just like Lorelei. As a precaution, I dropped a sleep charm on the lamia as well, even though she was still unconscious.

Then Winnie held up the whistle. "Nanu Nakula, who is your master now?"

The mongoose leaned exhausted against her leg, chest heaving from his incredible effort. "You are . . . ," he puffed, "O kindest . . . and best of masters."

Winnie pointed at the fire around Lorelei. "I wish for enough water to put out the flames but only that much."

"Then water you shall have," the mongoose said.

He was a blur again, and soon there was no blaze, only a puddle of water on the floor and the mongoose standing to the side with a sooty teacup in his paws.

"Well, that's done," Winnie said, dusting off her

hands. She glanced at her ring and smiled, as if what she saw pleased her.

Rowan, though, gave a sigh. "I wish I could take care of all my other problems this easy."

"It'll be quite a feather in your cap when you report Lorelei to the Council." I nodded to the kobolds and the lamia. "I daresay Lorelei and her crew of thugs are behind a lot of other crimes."

"How long will the Council put them in jail?" Winnie wanted to know.

I shook my head. "The Council has no jails. It will be cheaper and easier to wipe their memories and then place a compulsion upon them to stay away from San Francisco and never think of whistles, mongooses, or wishes again."

Rowan shifted uncomfortably. "I'm afraid that I'll have to bring in the mongoose and whistle too. The Council will probably want to change the mongoose into his pendant form, where he can't make trouble."

The mongoose had been licking the burnt spots on his fur. He looked up in alarm. "Was I not Helpful! Why can I not stay that way?"

Winnie scooped him up in her hands. "How could you do that to him? He saved our lives."

Rowan slapped his hands helplessly against his sides.

"I know, and I'm sorry. But what if someone worse than Lorelei stole the whistle and wished for an army of monsters or a warehouse full of bombs?"

Winnie made a nasal buzzing sound. "Wrong. Nanu Nakula would never let a wish get out of hand like that. The Heart of Kubera had a lot of other masters, and no one created a monster army."

"That doesn't mean someone won't wish it in the future," Rowan said unhappily. "As long as you have the Heart of Kubera, you'll be a magnet for every power-hungry villain."

Winnie folded her arms confidently. "Miss Drake will protect me like she always does."

"Not even Miss Drake could keep away all the evil creatures who will want the whistle," Rowan said, and looked at me. "And she knows it."

I cleared my throat. "The real problem is that the mongoose has no free will. He must grant the wishes of whoever has the whistle. So the Council will want to prevent that."

Winnie stroked the mongoose. "I'm not going to let that happen."

She didn't see the mongoose as a wish-fulfilling machine but as a small creature who needed her help. So she was ready to defy even me. I'd wished for her to be as caring as her great-grandfather, but this wasn't quite what I'd had in mind. "You may not have any choice in the matter either."

"Choice," she murmured, and bit her lip thoughtfully. "The problem is that he has to do what his master tells him. But what if I could arrange it so he doesn't?"

"You mean if he has free will? Well, the Council might relent," I said, "but how are you going to do that?"

"The Heart of Kubera doesn't belong to me or Lorelei or anyone. He belongs to himself." She held the whistle in one hand. "Will you help me change this into a piece of fudge?"

I shook my head. "Disguising the whistle won't fool the Council."

"That's not what I have in mind," she said, and thrust her hand toward me. "Please."

Even though I didn't think it would do any good, I was curious to see what my pet was planning. It took me a moment to work on a spell and a muttered chant, and a few signs later, the whistle had become a big lump of fudge.

Winnie looked down at the mongoose on her palm. "Do you want to stay Helpful?"

The mongoose's head bobbed up and down. "Oh, yes. More than ever."

She held the fudge in front of his muzzle. "Then eat this."

I thought it would take him a while to eat the fudge, but he downed it in three gulps, cheeks bulging.

"The whistle's inside you now." Winnie grinned at him. "So that makes you your own master. The only wishes you have to grant are your own."

Proud of Winnie, I put my paw on her shoulder. Not many creatures would give up that power or that potential wealth, so perhaps Winnie would take after Caleb after all. But if she didn't, that was also fine. No two pets grow up exactly alike. I'll continue to encourage the best qualities I find in her.

Smiling at the mongoose, I couldn't help gloating. "Ha! Have fun twisting your own commands."

He scratched his head in puzzlement. "What do I do now?" he asked with a faint whistle to his voice.

I suppose that after all these centuries it was hard to stop thinking like a servant. "Whatever you want? Go for a walk. Read a book. Take a nap." I pointed at the real gold coins, some of which were covered by a mess of chocolate and burnt feathers. "Though the Council might appreciate it if you might return the gold coins and valuables before anyone notices they're missing."

"But the rules do not say I have to clean up a mess," he protested.

"There are no rules for you anymore, Nanu," I said. "That's the point."

He folded his paws. "Yes, I suppose there are not," he said, sounding a little scared.

The next moment, he became a tan blur again, and the gold coins steadily disappeared. And when the last bit of treasure was gone, so was he.

Picking up three Golden Gate Bridge paperweights, Winnie tossed them one by one into the air, then caught them and flung them up again. Juggling sometimes helped calm her when she was feeling anxious. "Do you think he'll return?" Winnie asked.

"I hope not," I said fervently, and then instructed Rowan, "Now that the Heart of Kubera can choose to do good or evil, tell the Council that the mongoose is no worse and no better than any other powerful magical creature. If they lock him away, they'll also have to lock up every magical, including themselves."

Rowan scratched his head with his twisted fingers. "I guess it's for the best. I owe him my life after all. When I turn in Lorelei and her gang, I'll also tell my superiors that the mongoose is no longer a threat . . . due to your actions."

"Ask your aunt, Lady Louhi, to put in a good word for him too," I suggested.

He nodded and then turned to Winnie. "You're smart, but one day you're going to take one chance too many and it's going to get you in real trouble."

She just laughed. "That's already happened. I'm like Miss Drake that way."

....

ᴄᴧ⁓ Winnie ⌐⁓ᴧ

With a spell on Lorelei and the kobolds, my ring had returned to its normal self, only changing color in indoor or outdoor light. I told Miss Drake about the eagle I had seen in it that had given me the idea for my perfect wish.

"Ah," she said. "Colors to warn you. Shapes to aid you. The ring has many powers you can learn to use. It is beginning to bond with you, Winnie."

I was going to ask her if it could warn me when a dragon was in a bad mood, but I had a feeling if I did, my dragon's mood would turn bad right away.

A few days after we caught Lorelei, Mom's cattle drive ended, so I was able to call and tell her all about my latest adventure with Miss Drake. Of all the amazing things that had happened, including traveling into the past, battling monsters, and finding a fabulous ruby, what most impressed her was that I had met Great-Granddad Caleb.

"Miss Drake says there's a plaque downtown recognizing his work," I said. "I think I'd like to see it and discover more about him."

"So would I," she agreed. "I could never get my father to talk about my grandfather."

"Then it's a date," I said. When I turned off my phone, though, I noticed that my hands had turned bright pink. Even my ring was pink. Hurrying into my bathroom, I checked the mirror. My face and hair had changed to the same color too. I looked like a flamingo.

Leaning my head against the mirror, I gave a big sigh. "Well, you got me, Sir Isaac." I had no idea how he had done it, but it was going to be awfully embarrassing when I went to school the next day.

I scrubbed my face with soap and water as hard as I could, but my cheeks stayed pink. So I went to ask Miss Drake for help. If she couldn't do anything, I guess I could wear a sign to school saying that I'd been pranked by Sir Isaac. It would save a lot of explanations.

I found her in the living room having tea with Rowan.

"I was just about to get you, Winn—good heavens! Why did you dye yourself that alarming shade of pink?"

"Sir Isaac did this to me." I didn't have to explain about the revenge pranking. Miss Drake knew all about Sir Isaac's sense of humor. "Can you make me less flamingo-y?"

"I'll see what I can do after our guests leave," Miss Drake said, always the proper host.

I was going to ask who else was here beside Rowan, when the mongoose suddenly sprang out of a teacake in a spray of crumbs and powdered sugar and landed on my shoulder.

"Hel-lo, former master," he said.

I stroked a finger along his fur. "Are you moving into our attic again?"

Miss Drake reared her head. "He most certainly is not. The Council has decided that he needs to be under Lady Louhi's supervision, so he'll be staying with her and Rowan."

"I can still visit you, though," Nanu Nakula added.

"But not often." Miss Drake held up a claw. "Remember: Absence makes the heart grow fonder, so I'll be fonder of you the longer you stay away." She glanced at the clock on the mantle. "Ah, nearly sunset." She stretched her wings open a little and wriggled her shoulders to loosen her muscles. "I feel like a little exercise. Rowan, have you ever flown?"

"No," he admitted. "Not even in an airplane."

I twisted my head to look at the mongoose. "How about you?"

The mongoose began to bob up and down excitedly. "I was Beautiful when a former master rode a flying carpet, but I have never flown as Helpful."

Miss Drake rose. "Then let's go for a little flight."

Rowan offered his palm to the mongoose. "Hop on board."

I felt a little jealous as the mongoose jumped from my shoulder and onto his hand. Then, sliding Nanu Nakula into his shirt pocket, Rowan rose to get his coat from the hall closet.

He'd worn a thick one when he visited us, so we didn't have to find something warm for him. All I would need was my magical scarf.

He looked at it doubtfully. "That's not going to be enough to keep you from getting cold."

I wound it around my neck. "I'll be warmer than you. This is made from the wool of ice sheep."

Miss Drake joined us in human form, and we walked over to the nearby hospital and rode the elevator up to the roof. Then she transformed herself and cast her invisibility spell to keep naturals from seeing us. "Can we go to Clipper's?" I asked. "She's got everything, so I bet she even has toys and clothes for a mongoose."

"No, we're returning to the marina today," Miss Drake said as she hunkered down on the roof and spread her wings.

I climbed on first and Rowan got on after me. Then, with a great flap of her wings, we soared up into the air, curving over the hills. The sun was low on the horizon, painting the waters of the bay with flaming oranges and yellows and reds as it drifted down toward the Golden Gate.

In the afternoon, winds swept across the Marina Green, so it was the best place to fly kites, and today there were lots of huge ones floating in the air. And they were all such funny shapes—yachts, castles, limousines, giant puffins, coaches, and even a gazebo, each of them hovering in one spot like they were glued to the sky.

The only one whipping around in the breeze was a little paper diamond kite that a kid was flying from below. Then I saw that the others didn't even have a string attaching them to the ground or anyone to handle the strings in the first place.

Willamar leaned from a gazebo, which tilted dangerously as he began to wave. "Welcome, welcome. We've been waiting for our guests of honor." He stared at me and then tried to be polite. "And . . . uh . . . may I say what a lovely shade of pink you are, Miss Winnie."

A purple-and-black pumpkin-shaped carriage glided next to us, and Silana looked through the window. "*Très chic.* I'm sure you'll make pink all the rage at Spriggs tomorrow."

I groaned inside because she'd tell her niece, Nanette, tonight, which would give my foe plenty of time to come up with insults for the next morning.

Then, from all the other floating objects, the Fellowship of the Jewel City began calling their greetings as well as compliments on my pinkness because they thought I'd done it intentionally. I was so embarrassed I would have stayed pink even if Sir Isaac ended his prank right this moment.

With a sigh, I asked Miss Drake, "Won't someone notice all this stuff in the sky?"

Miss Drake arched her head over her back to grin at us. "I believe they're invisible to naturals, or Rowan will have to report all of us."

"I'm glad it won't come to that," he said.

"After our flight, we'll descend to my boat for refreshments." Willamar pointed to a large catamaran with a gold and silver castle on its deck. "And of course, we'd all like to meet the Heart of Kubera at last."

"The news got around about Nanu Nakula?" I asked Miss Drake.

"There are Council members who also belong to the Fellowship. They heard my report," Rowan explained.

The mongoose poked his head from inside Rowan's coat. "I'm hungry. When do we eat?"

"Soon. Now, behave," Miss Drake said.

Standing on the small deck at the stern of a long, shallow boat, Sir Isaac used a long pole to guide it through the air toward us. "How clever of you, Burton. You're color-coordinated with the sunset."

I held up my arm and saw it was the same shade as part of the sky. "Are we even, Sir Isaac?"

"My honor is satisfied so the answer is yes." He raised his straw hat in one hand and the pole in the other. "Huzzah! The war is over, and peace reigns supreme once again."

"Sir Isaac," I asked, trying to sound as humble and polite as I could, "how did you do it?"

He set his hat on his head again. "That would be telling, Burton. But in class tomorrow, we will learn how to remove pinkness."

And, I thought, it will also be a lesson to my classmates about what happens when you try to trick Sir Isaac.

Sir Isaac's eyes twinkled. "And if you carefully watch

each step of your de-pinking, Burton, you may be able to work out the process in reverse. And then you too can pink-ify anyone you like."

I put my hands up. "Anyone but you. I learned my lesson."

"Sir Isaac, we don't want to lose the light," Lady Louhi said, and then greeted us and Rowan. "Come join us, Rowan. You'll appreciate Sir Isaac's new gizmo."

She was sitting in the prow, and between her and Sir Isaac was a machine with lots of copper wires, brass coils, and lights. On the very top was a globe about the size of a softball. Miss Drake glided close, and Rowan, with Nanu Nakula, easily leapt down to Lady Louhi's boat.

"What's happening?" I asked.

Sir Isaac waved one arm in a flourish. "With the Council's kind permission, we're going to re-create our own Jewel City. My task will be to gather the raw materials, and Lady Louhi's will be to shape it. And then Old Sol will paint them in suitable hues." He turned to her. "Shall we begin, my lady?"

When Lady Louhi nodded, Sir Isaac threw a brass switch. The next instant, the machine shuddered, and the vibrations made the boat bob up and down. Sir Isaac steadied it with his pole. When the device fell into a steady hum, I felt like hundreds of ants were crawling over my skin.

Always the teacher, Sir Isaac called to me, "The sensation you're feeling is caused by atoms gathering and forming into water molecules." The air began to grow drizzly, and then beneath us clouds began to form, merging into one long sheet that hid even the city's tallest buildings beneath it—and all of us from the city. It looked like one long layer of cookie dough that the setting sun dyed orange and rose.

At the same time, Lady Louhi had been whispering a spell, careful to keep her hands hidden inside the boat as she drew her signs. Miss Drake soared left and I waved, but I could see Rowan and Nanu Nakula were already occupied, fascinated by the whirring gizmo.

When Lady Louhi finished, misty columns began to rise like plant stalks, and the tops of the columns swelled into domes and roofs like flowers blossoming. I began to recognize some of the buildings I'd seen like the Palace of Fine Arts, and of course I couldn't miss the outline of the Tower of Jewels. The breeze made their cottony sides sway like they were alive and breathing, and the sun colored them in pinks and oranges and greens and blues. And the moisture sparkled so that each building seemed to be outlined in glittering gems.

It was almost as lovely as the magnificent Jewel City that had once stood below us, a wonderful and beautiful fair I would never forget.

227

Sir Isaac cupped his free hand around his mouth like a megaphone. "Everybody, you have ten minutes, and then the illusion will have to disperse. So enjoy!"

Miss Drake soared up high and then began gliding westward across the cloudy Persian carpet of delights. "I think Mrs. Wilder would have loved this," I said.

"So would Caleb," she agreed.

As we glided about the regal Tower of Jewels, I thought of how it stood out from the rest just like Laura Ingalls Wilder and Caleb had. "I'd like to do something that counted like they did."

Miss Drake arched her long neck, and the setting sun made her scales glow crimson red. But she was beautiful in any light. "You will, my dear. That's one wish we don't need the Heart of Kubera for. We'll make it come true ourselves."

I put my arms around her and pressed my face right against her scales. They were dry, cool, strong. "You are my wish come true."

Miss Drake nuzzled her cheek against me. "And you are mine."

And we went on gliding through that city of light and dreams.

AFTERWORD

Without Laura Ingalls Wilder, we would never have written this book. So, in her honor and as an homage, we wished her to be part of it.

In 1915, forty-eight-year-old Laura Ingalls Wilder traveled by train from Missouri to visit her daughter, Rose Wilder Lane, and to see San Francisco and the Panama-Pacific International Exposition, known as the PPIE. At the time, she and her husband, Almanzo, were farmers, and she occasionally wrote for local newspapers about rural life and raising her chickens.

"I intend to try to do some writing that will count," she wrote to her "Manly." And she did—she wrote many more articles, and then many years later, books based on her own childhood—the Little House books—that have delighted and inspired generations of young readers.

In the 1970s, when I was a young editor at Harper &

Row, I helped edit the book *West from Home: Letters of Laura Ingalls Wilder, San Francisco, 1915*. I was a New Yorker through and through, but I had been to San Francisco and had, like many others, left my heart there. So Laura Ingalls Wilder's lively and affectionate descriptions of the city, the ocean, and her introduction to this marvelous fair won me over. I wished I could travel back in time to see the PPIE too.

The PPIE celebrated the completion and opening of the Panama Canal and especially the revival and rebirth of San Francisco from the destruction caused by the 1906 earthquake and great fire. San Franciscans were ready to show the world their city was flourishing again. The fair was spectacular, full of inventions, amazing machines, aeronautics, and the best art, culture, food, and fun that the world could offer.

Larry is a San Francisco native, and when I left New York to be with him, we settled there for over a decade. In 2015, we joined in the festivities celebrating the hundredth anniversary of the PPIE. We decided to write a story so Winnie could visit this wonderful fair and, through her, so could our readers. We imagined Winnie briefly meeting her beloved author and being able to tell her how much she enjoyed her books . . . though to Laura Ingalls Wilder they were still just a wish and a dream. Laura was courageous and curious, like Winnie, and we felt that if ever they did meet, they might be kindred spirits.

The PPIE opened on February 20, 1915, and closed on December 4, 1915. Our descriptions include activities and sites throughout the time of the Exposition.

Joanne Ryder

Serendipity is part of writing. Joanne introduced me to the Rubin Museum of Art in New York. There I saw the most wonderful statue of the potbellied Kubera, the Hindu and Buddhist god of wealth. He was grinning as he squeezed his mongoose like a tube of toothpaste—only what came out of his pet's mouth was a stream of jewels. While Kubera has numerous names, forms, and attributes, he not only grants riches, but according to the museum, he and his mongoose remind people to be equally generous and selfless. The statue was my inspiration for the Heart of Kubera—a mongoose with a ruby heart.

Laurence Yep

SOME RECOMMENDED SOURCES ABOUT THE SAN FRANCISCO FAIR OF 1915

Wilder, Laura Ingalls. *West from Home: Letters of Laura Ingalls Wilder, San Francisco, 1915*. Edited by Roger Lea MacBride. HarperCollins Publishers, 1974.

Written long before her Little House books, Laura's letters to her husband convey her personal impressions of San Francisco and the 1915 Fair. These early letters will charm her fans with glimpses of her life and aspirations as a writer.

Ackley, Laura A. *San Francisco's Jewel City: The Panama-Pacific International Exposition of 1915*. Heyday, 2014.

Elaborately illustrated and carefully researched, this is an excellent and well-written guide for anyone interested in the 1915 fair and its background.

Bruno, Lee. *Panorama: Tales of the 1915 Pan-Pacific International Exposition*. Cameron + Company, 2014.

A coffee-table book with photographs, helpful maps, and stories of the 1915 Fair.

Lieber, Robert, and Sarah Lau, editors. *The Last Great World's Fair: San Francisco Panama-Pacific International Exposition 1915.* Golden Gate National Parks Conservancy, 2004.

An overview of the Fair, including hand-tinted photographs and fascinating firsts and facts.

ONLINE SOURCES

Panama-Pacific International Exposition. ppie100.org

This website of the 2015 centennial celebration in San Francisco and vicinity contains a wealth of information about the original Fair.

Macomber, Ben. *The Jewel City: Its Planning and Achievements; Its Architecture, Sculpture, Symbolism, and Music; Its Gardens, Palaces, and Exhibits.* San Francisco, 1915. http://www.archive.org/details/jewelcityitspla02macogoog

Much of this material originally appeared as articles in the San Francisco Chronicle. Written at the time of the Exposition, it includes detailed descriptions of the 1915 Fair buildings, courtyards, artwork, illuminations, and exhibits.